SOMEWHERE IN SAN DIEGO

SOMEWHERE IN
SAN DIEGO

DENNIS MACARAEG

SOMEWHERE IN SAN DIEGO

Cover Design by M.S. Fowle

Interior book design by Pen 2 Ink Designs

For my son,
Kevin Macaraeg

ONE

DANNY MAGLAYA SWEPT HIS EYES from side to side looking for a place to hide.

Though it was a perfect day—the sun rising in the clear blue San Diego sky—his predicament was far from perfect.

He peeked over his shoulder and saw a windowless van steadily following him along North Harbor Drive. Two men, dressed in black tactical pants and dark green t-shirts, were inside. Armed with assault rifles, Danny knew they were after one thing: the only copy of a thumb drive containing data from ships assigned to track the progress of Rx-18. Danny had invented RX-18, a compound that attracts prized ocean fish, with help from fellow marine biologist Blake Mason.

If he didn't outrun the men in the van, it would be his last day on earth.

Danny needed to meet up with Blake to send the information on the thumb drive to kidnappers holding Blake's fiancée, Elizabeth, as hostage, in exchange for her freedom.

Blake and Danny wanted to upload its entirety from the main server of their company, SDM Biosciences, but when

Blake was searching for the folders where the information was stored, he found that the data had been wiped clean. Blake called Danny immediately about the situation. Luckily, Danny had saved a backup copy on the thumb drive.

For the information to be uploaded to the server that the kidnappers demanded, he and Blake would have to do it through his company's secure computer system. But that was out of the question. The perimeter of his company's campus was crawling with men wanting to stop the two from completing the task. His only hope was to join up with Blake who was carrying a dedicated laptop that could upload the information.

Danny and Blake were given exactly 36 hours to meet their demand or else Elizabeth would be drowned. They had already wasted three.

As Danny ran for his life, he wondered just who the men chasing him were. They couldn't be the same people who had kidnapped Elizabeth—it just didn't make any sense. Why did they want to take the thumb drive away from him, since it was impossible for anyone to access the data? Only Danny and Blake could do it through the ten-digit passcode and finger scan. It had to be a group that didn't want the information on the thumb drive uploaded, he reasoned. But what for? It only contained data regarding the fish migrations from tuna breeding grounds in the Pacific Ocean to the protected waters of the Pacific Rim designated as fishing-free zones.

But none of that mattered right now, Danny thought. His top priority was to rendezvous with Blake so they could complete the task and free Elizabeth.

Uploading the files was supposed to have been easy, but now, as Danny ran for his life, he wished he hadn't designed the thumb drive with a complicated system that could be unlocked only through a dedicated computer—so he didn't have to go through all the trouble he was in.

He scanned his surroundings. Immediately he spotted the massive San Diego City and County Administration Building. He thought of hiding inside and calling Blake from his phone. To do that, he'd have to cross a wide street, including a center island lined with palm trees, while cars zoomed past. If he chose that option, he'd be exposed and the men chasing him would definitely spot him right away.

He dropped the idea.

Out of the corner of his eye, the Star of India caught his attention—a tall sailing ship built in the nineteenth century, moored at a dock along the waterfront. Its two main masts reached for the clouds floating by, gently rocking with the motion of the water.

The sailing ship reminded him of the Manila Galleons that sailed the Pacific Ocean from the late 1500s to the early 1800s. The ships carrying silks, porcelains, spices and other riches from the Philippines traveled all the way to Monterey then headed south to Acapulco—bypassing San Diego.

He thought of running up the gangplank, then onto the deck to hide deep within the bowels of its iron hull. Seeing there was a group of young students already waiting in line to get on the ship, he decided against it. The men in the van wouldn't hesitate to shoot him in plain sight of the children.

He kept running.

THE MAN IN THE PASSENGER seat, his long black hair tied back into a ponytail, rolled down his tinted window and turned to the driver. "Where the fuck is this guy?!"

"One o'clock. The tall Filipino guy. Can't you see him?"

Ponytail half-smiled as he cocked the AR-15 resting on his lap, popped the rear sight up, and aligned his aim with the front sight. With steady hands, he pointed his weapon at Danny's back. Without wasting another second, he pulled the trigger.

DANNY WAS NEARING THE USS Midway Museum when he heard the cracks of machine gun fire. From his position, the *rat-a-tat-tat* staccato burst sounded like firecrackers on the Fourth of July.

The projectiles hit the bench next to him, splitting the wooden backrest and sending splinters flying in every direction. The sight sent chills up his spine.

Reacting quickly to the fluid situation, and not thinking about the possibility of getting injured, Danny dove forward as bullets flew past his head. His elbows scraped against the rough concrete surface. He rolled to his side and crouched behind a large concrete tree planter.

He turned his head to his left. The black van was approaching him, this time at high-speed.

A burst of bullets exploded once more. The smoldering ballistics coming at him were relentless, sending chunks of the concrete pathway flying left and right. Out of the corner of his eye, Danny saw a line of sparks. He moved his leg away just before his femur would have been shattered by the onslaught of copper coming at him.

A panicked woman in a tank top began dialing 9-1-1. With the police patrolling nearby, the last thing Danny wanted was to be detained and interrogated as to why he was being shot at. Five—maybe ten hours of questioning would be wasted before he could be released. It would undoubtedly lead to Elizabeth's demise. He quickly got up and dashed away with the rest of the fleeing tourists, hoping to blend in like a chameleon and never to be seen again.

Flashing red and blue police lights converged at the north end of Seaport Village. There must have been at least half-dozen squad cars speeding towards the panicked pedestrians as they ran for their lives. At least the men in the van would back off. The thought of it gave him a temporary relief.

Finding no place to hide, he scanned the horizon. Danny was glad to see the familiar statue of a sailor kissing a nurse, modeled after the iconic Times Square V-J Day photo. He hid behind one of the sailor's massive legs.

Just then, his phone beeped signaling an incoming email. He pulled it out from his pocket. To his horror, he saw Elizabeth's picture, standing inside a glass tank with the water up to her ankles; her ocean blue eyes in sheer panic. The message underneath read, "The water rises another two inches every hour. She will be completely submerged if the data is not uploaded by exactly 7 p.m. tomorrow."

He dialed Blake's number.

"Where are you?" Danny shouted into the microphone connected to his earphones.

"I'm by the carousel," Blake responded, urgency in his voice.

"Did you see her picture?"

"Yes . . . just several minutes ago. I'll be there in eight minutes. We need to end this now."

Danny shut his phone and dropped it into his front pocket. As he ran towards Seaport Village, he caught one more glimpse of the police cars and ambulances attending to the shocked bystanders.

Two

Teeming with tourist activities, Seaport Village resembled a small village with a collection of harbor side shops and restaurants. As Danny hurried to get to Blake, wanting to end their nightmarish situation as soon as possible, he ran past tourists walking briskly along the waterfront with hot mochas in their hands. Danny was glad that Blake chose the pedestrian-only location to meet. The men in the black van wouldn't see them amidst the crowd.

Visitors from all over the world were soaking up the warm California sun—oblivious to the police activity just less than a quarter mile away. Mothers pushed their baby strollers at a leisurely pace. A woman in a tank top and runner's shorts jogged past him, her hair swinging from side to side. Teenagers ate giant pretzels sprinkled with crystal-sized salt, sitting atop the white wall, laughing without a trouble in the world. He wished he could have a regular day like them, but the reality of his situation was quite different. As vines of worry steadfastly grew from the pit of his stomach, he knew better. With each passing minute, Danny and

Blake's situation seemed to get worse. All he wanted was to get to his best friend and save Elizabeth, not to mention just surviving this horrendous day.

He shot a glance at a restaurant's big bay window. Just two days ago, Danny's life was as normal as anyone else's. He was there with Blake and some of his other fellow scientists having a lunch meeting and discussing the next phase in their project. He was enjoying freshly shucked oysters topped with a few drops of hot sauce and a squeeze of lemon, with smoked salmon on the side. That seemed trivial now because the men chasing him could capture either him or Blake at any moment and take the thumb drive away.

Arriving at the carousel, a smile of relief spread across Danny's face when he saw Blake waiting by one of the tables under white parasols. From a distance, Danny could see the excitement painted on Blake's face. Danny felt confident that in less than five minutes the data demanded by the kidnappers would already have been uploaded to their server. Then Elizabeth's location would be texted to them, and the whole dreadful situation would be over.

While Danny was taking long strides towards Blake, he heard the loud thumping of boots thudding against the pavement. Danny shot a look to where the manic steps were coming from. To his shock, he saw a bald man in black fatigues, a tattoo of a snake's head on the side of his neck protruding from his dark green T-shirt. The man charged at him, groping for the gun tucked in his waistband.

Danny waved his hands. Just as Blake turned his head to investigate what was going on, bullets began flying all over the place. A middle-aged couple taking pictures dropped their camera while running away from the man firing indiscriminately.

Blake grabbed the umbrella in front of him, using it as a cloaking device, and hid behind the table so the shooter couldn't see which side of the umbrella he was hiding behind. Danny could still hear the entire clip being emptied. The man was intent on killing Blake. A hollow-point bullet flew past Blake's chest, missing the side of his ribcage by mere centimeters. Soda cans and French fries sitting on the table exploded, the soda spilling down his back and fries raining down upon him, ketchup smearing his shirt.

Danny had to do something quick if he wanted to see his friend live through the day. He searched his immediate area for a weapon to stop the man from slaughtering his best friend. Spotting a walking cane resting on the wall in front of a nearby gift shop, he dashed for it.

THE BALD MAN RAN OUT of bullets. He ejected the clip. The empty magazine made a clinking sound as it hit the concrete surface of the food court. Wasting no time, he reached for another magazine tucked in his pocket.

CAPITALIZING ON THE LULL IN the mayhem, Danny galloped towards Baldy. He smashed the hard, wooden cane into the man's wrist. The pistol flew out from the man's hand. Danny followed up with an upward swing, jamming the tip of the cane into the man's chin. He then followed up with an immediate thrust to the man's stomach. The man doubled over and fell on his knees as the pain knifed through his abdomen. Danny continued his assault, smashing the cane directly into the man's shoulder with the intent to disable him so that he and Blake could run away. Hurting someone was the last thing Danny wanted, but he had no choice. He had to stop this animal from slaughtering Blake or himself. With the thin blade of his hand, Danny followed up with a hard karate chop to the side of his neck.

Baldy fell forward, smashing his face into the hard surface.

"Who sent you?!" Danny shouted, pressing the full weight of his right knee into the man's right thigh.

"Fuck you!" the man grunted as he gasped for air.

"Tell me who, you piece of shit!" Danny screamed.

"Forget about him!" Blake interrupted, concern trembling in his voice. "He doesn't matter. We need to upload the data right now."

Blake had a point, Danny realized. Interrogating the man wasn't their top priority. Precious time was being wasted. He released the man. Danny was rising from his knees to get to the table where the laptop was sitting, when suddenly he and Blake heard tires screeching. Danny searched where the distant sound was coming from. It was the windowless van that had been chasing him earlier. The driver-side door opened, and the man with the ponytail bolted out, an AR-15 in his hands.

"We need to get out of here!" Blake yelled.

Danny ran towards the Marina, not sure where to go or where he could hide. Blake cleared the carousel area and sprinted to the parking lot.

DASHING AS FAST AS HE could along the marina, Danny caught a glimpse of the gray U.S. Navy aircraft carriers docked at the pier on North Island. The sight he captured gave a clear picture of why San Diego is called a Navy town: Home of the Pacific Fleet in the U.S. Mainland.

He wondered how he would evade the men who were just yards behind him. He eyed the cozy shops selling soaps and souvenir items. He thought of hiding in one of them to wait it out until the two men were gone. He scuttled the idea. It was too risky. If he was seen, there wasn't a chance he could defend himself against the high-powered weapons the two assassins were carrying. He kept running, passing a boy and his father flying a kite on the green grass.

Danny eventually arrived at the foot of the wide steps leading up to the San Diego Convention Center. The structure's roof, made of white fabric which resembled sails of a seagoing ship, reflected the bright sun. He contemplated if going up the stairs and then down the other side to disappear onto Harbor Drive's wide boulevard was a good plan. Apprehension dripping down his temples, he guessed that the two men were probably fanning out, and one of them might already be waiting for him at the other side.

Just then, he remembered a speedboat was tied up nearby—the one that his company used when conducting research off the tip of Point Loma. The men chasing him might have already called for reinforcements, and the place could be crawling with them by now—there was no place to hide. Getting to the speedboat and to open water was his only chance of escape.

He inspected the walkways for any sign of the men looking for him. Confident that the coast was clear, Danny scrambled to the locked gate a few blocks away.

Punching the combination into the electronic keypad, he heard the sweet sound of the lock clicking open.

Boat owners sat on the deck with their locally brewed beers, watching Danny with curiosity as he flew down the ramp.

Finding the speedboat, he untied it and jumped in. He kicked the speedboat away from the dock.

"IGOR, THE MOTHERFUCKER IS OVER there!" the one with a ponytail shouted, pointing to Danny.

Igor (i.e., Baldy) pulled the gate handle hard trying to force it open, but it wouldn't budge. Not even bothering to override the lock, he unclipped the gun from his waistband and fired several shots directly into the latch. The lock shattered, sending pieces of metals crashing into the ground.

Igor pulled the door handle once more and the gate flew open.

"Yuri, we need to steal a boat!"

SWITCHING THE PROPELLER INTO REVERSE, Danny's boat pulled away from the marina. He shot a quick glance behind him. To his dismay, the men who wanted him dead were already speeding down the dock. Danny shifted the propeller again, picking up forward speed. Finding room to safely get out, he pointed the speedboat towards the bay. As soon as he had floated far from the inlet, he pushed the throttle further. The outboard engine screamed for mercy as it took in more air and gas, pushing the tachometer needle close to the red line. The front of the watercraft tilted upwards as if intending to fly, gliding across the smooth water away from the rest of the moored boats. He aimed for Coronado Island hoping to find safety.

YURI SEARCHED THE AREA FOR a vessel to commandeer. A sly smile came to his face when he saw a man on a boat similar to Danny's with the engine already on idle. He made eye contact with Igor and pointed to the clueless man.

Igor jumped on the boat and shoved the man away from the steering wheel. Startled by the sudden invasion, the man grabbed Igor by the shirt intending to push him away from his boat. Yuri jumped in, wrapped his massive arms around the man's neck, and pulled him away from Igor.

As soon as Igor regained his composure, he grasped the man by his legs. The man kicked and thrashed his arms violently to get the two strangers off of him, but he was no match for Yuri and Igor's savagery. They threw the man overboard without any regard for his safety. With the boat in their possession, they took off after Danny.

WANTING TO KNOW IF HE was in the clear, Danny looked back, his hands on the steering wheel guiding the watercraft away from the marina. The sight of the two men chasing him didn't look good as the high-performance speedboat gained distance on him real fast. The wind pressed hard on his face, loudly swirling in his ears. Trying to get his bearings, he squinted his eyes away from the bright ivory sun as it illuminated the troubled water with thousands of tiny sparkles. Relieved that Coronado Island was just a short distance away, he stayed the course.

As he was surveying for a spot to park his boat with a suitable place to flee, he heard the popping sounds of automatic gunfire. His stomach dropped from sheer terror, knowing bullets could pierce the boat's hull, or even hit the gas tank and turn the boat into a ball of flame. He looked back. His fear was confirmed as he saw Igor's shaved head bobbing just above the topaz-colored seawater.

YURI FOLLOWED THE TRAIL OF the wake that Danny's boat had left behind. Igor pointed the AR-15 at the speedboat, peered through the sights, and emptied the magazine. The automatic rifle spat out bullets at a rapid rate. The windshield shattered, sending shards of glass flying in all directions. Danny ducked his head and placed his arm in front of his face.

Desperate to take evasive action, Danny spun the steering wheel to the left. The boat violently turned, spraying salty gray water to the side. His hip jerked to the right from the powerful G-force, and he lost his footing. The side of the boat hit a rising swell, cutting the forward momentum. His hands slipped off the steering wheel, and he was thrown to the side. He got on his knees and started to crawl back to the driver's seat when another wave slammed the bottom of the boat's hull, sending him airborne.

The speedboat landed on the water hard throwing him all the way to the aft and tossing him out of the boat. With quick thinking, he grabbed the side of the vessel, clawing at the railings. But the rushing water made his grip slippery. Mustering all his strength, he threw his left leg over the side and pulled himself back inside the hull.

DANNY COULD MAKE OUT THE shapes of the U.S. Navy ships at NAS North Island, but with the seawater splashing in his face, it was hard to steer the boat to the nearest dock. He thought of going to the base to seek the protection of the shore patrols. But just as the idea crossed his mind, he rejected it right away. The military would definitely arrest him for trespassing a secure military installation and call the local police.

Danny desperately scanned Coronado's shores. The island was roughly seven square miles but it was almost impossible to find a place to park his boat. He caught a glimpse of the Coronado Ferry Landing. Docking the boat at the pier and running up the gangplank for his escape was his only option.

But he was dismayed to see a ferry full of passengers at the Landing. He hadn't noticed it since he was more focused on getting away from the two men chasing him. Though the large boat was slower than his craft, it was already several feet away from the dock. He thought of squeezing himself between the ferry and the dock but worried that he wouldn't be able to stop and slam head-on into the massive wooden pilings. If the two men chasing him did not kill him first, the impact would. Danny added more power and maneuvered around it. Trying to get to the Coronado Ferry Landing first was now a suicide move.

Out of the corner of his eye, he saw a small sandy cove.

He turned away, avoiding a head-on crash. Instead of cutting power, he shoved the throttle forward, redlining the tachometer. The speedboat's six-cylinder engine quadrupled its effort to move faster. In a matter of seconds, the boat's speed doubled. He pressed his back against the dashboard, held on to the railings, firmly planted his feet on the deck, and braced for impact.

The boat zoomed through the shallow water. A few seconds later, the boat's hull scraped its way into the white sandy cove. A deafening bang followed.

The boat stopped. Danny's stomach slammed against the steering wheel. Pain spread across his abdomen. He was thrown overboard, landing on his back. The boat tumbled end over end, stopping mere inches from his head. Though the force of the impact was intense, the sandy soil softened his landing. His head was shoved into the sand, covering his arms and face. Feeling no severe pain, he brushed himself off and stood up. A crowd gathered around him. A middle-aged Asian woman in a visor approached him, asking if he was OK. He raised his hand signaling all was well. As soon as he regained his composure, he sped to the nearby Marketplace shops hoping he wouldn't be found.

Anticipating that the two men would be there soon, Danny summed up all his available options. He considered waiting for a driver to get in a car and carjack him. Not only was it a desperate attempt to escape his quagmire, but it was also a terrible thought. Danny wasn't like that. Besides, with hundreds of people nearby, surely someone would have a cell phone and call the cops. He wouldn't even make it off of the island without being arrested. Swinging his head side to side, he saw a gift shop selling souvenirs. Not wanting to loiter outside any longer, he walked into the store. The place was bustling with foreigners and people from out of state. He heard voices with northeastern accents mingled with European languages he didn't understand. Hiding behind a tall rack of postcards, he peeked outside to check if the two goons were nearby.

His phone vibrated in his pocket. Glancing at the screen, he saw that it was Blake. He pushed the headphones back into his ears, then immediately pressed the inline microphone.

"Where are you?" Danny asked, worried for his friend's safety.

"I left downtown and am hiding somewhere I hope is safe. I can't tell you where for now. I don't trust our phones."

"Who are these men trying to kill us?"

"I really don't know. It seems they won't stop until they've got the thumb drive and the laptop," Blake declared in a rapid voice.

"We need to meet now so we can upload that data. We've got to save Elizabeth."

"We can't say anything over the phone. I'm pretty sure that these guys are listening to our conversation."

"How do you know that?" Danny asked perplexed.

"I just know. The field notes I dictated into my phone were deleted remotely," Blake declared. "Did you see Elizabeth's latest picture?"

"I just did earlier. This is terrible," Danny commented, distress in his voice. "If that's the case, should we communicate through one of those encrypted apps?"

"We can't. I don't trust our phones anymore. I'm sure we've already been hacked, and we're being monitored from each keystroke we make to every time we talk."

"We have to think of something real quick or Elizabeth will be dead!" Danny responded, now sounding frantic.

"We have to think this through. We only have one chance of making things right. Even with a simple mistake, we're all finished."

Just then, Danny saw his attackers walk past the gift shop.

"Gotta go. I just saw the two guys chasing me. I need to get somewhere safe," Danny said, turning off his phone right away.

He proceeded directly to the T-shirt rack and picked out a dark blue hoodie with "San Diego" in bold lettering, along with a cheap pair of sunglasses. Not wasting precious time, he proceeded to the cashier to pay.

The cashier, a young woman with short blonde hair, smiled at him as she scanned the items. "The sunglasses are on special. They're buy one, get one free."

"No thanks," Danny responded. Apprehension was palpable in his voice. "I only need one."

"It's really a good deal. You could give the extra pair to your girlfriend," the cashier insisted, clueless to the quandary he was in.

He glanced behind him and saw five customers with irritated looks on their faces. Not wanting to argue or cause a commotion and possibly attract the two men lurking outside, Danny smiled, grabbed a pair of sunglasses encrusted with fake plastic stones, and paid for his items.

As he exited the store, Danny wondered how he would get off the island without being detected. He slipped the hoodie on, donned the new pair of glasses, and flipped the hood over his head to conceal his face. Walking through the parking lot, he spotted Ponytail. He made a quick about-face to get away from him.

As he was coming around the bend, Yuri was getting closer. His attempt to escape wasn't fruitful. He was trapped. Thinking fast, he pulled his hoodie tighter to cover most of his face and pressed his sunglasses higher up with his thumb. He turned his head and peeked around the corner, anticipating how either of the men would react as soon he was detected.

Danny clenched his fist, ready to strike if the man jumped him.

Out of the corner of his eye, Danny noticed the ponytailed man moving swiftly towards his bald companion with measured steps. He wondered if the two men had already detected him and were formulating a plan to nab him.

As if the stars aligned in his favor, he was nearing a restaurant when a large group of patrons, talking and laughing loudly streamed out of the front door. Danny bowed his head, hunched over, and blended with them. As Baldy approached, he sidestepped and kept pace beside a man wearing a thin jacket, sandwiching himself between the unsuspecting patrons.

Concerned he might be discovered, Danny pulled out his cellphone from his pocket and pretended to be talking to conceal the side of his face. Inside the crowd, Danny became invisible.

Understanding that his magic act would only last a few minutes, he wished that he could snap his fingers, a spark of light would appear and he'd be gone in a flash and off the island.

But the only way he could get off the island was a ride out, but calling for a taxicab would compromise him. With his phone already monitored, the two men could be waiting for him at the taxi stand. He could go to one of the stores and ask to use the landline for a cab, but he was already far away from the shops. Trekking across the parking lot would expose him, and it could be suicide.

Danny was headed straight to the main street when he noticed a group of tourists standing in line to get on a double-decker tour bus. Patiently, he stood in the building's nook and waited for everyone to get on the bus.

As soon as the bus began moving, Danny chased after it. It was about to turn right into the street when he hopped onto a platform on the back, grasping ahold of the platform's handrail. Moving inside, he quickly squeezed himself between the other passengers. Danny spied through the glass window wanting to make sure that he was in the clear. The two men chasing him were standing in the middle of the parking lot, bewilderment on their faces.

Danny was thankful to see the Coronado Bridge straight ahead. He climbed up the steep stairs. Finding an empty seat, he rested his tired body. With the ends of his nerves sparking uncontrollably from what had just happened, he filled his lungs with the fresh ocean wind, trying to calm his tensed muscles. He repeated his slow breaths four times just as he had been taught in his martial arts training. He could have been captured or killed. Thankfully, the double-decker bus moved nonstop on the boomerang-shaped bridge leading back to downtown San Diego.

His phone vibrated. Eager to find out what Blake was planning to do, he fished it out of his front pocket with his thumb and forefinger.

"Hello," Danny answered, plugging his other ear to cut out the wind noise.

"Danny. I'm sure that the people chasing us know everything we're doing. I've come up with a plan that I think will work."

As Danny waited for what Blake was going to say, he wished that there was a unique language that only he or Blake could understand. Blake must have read his mind.

"You've heard of the code talkers in World War II, right?"

Blake's message puzzled Danny. He was lost with what Blake was trying to say.

"Neither one of us speak Navajo."

"I'm aware of that," Blake replied, frustration in his voice.

"We just have to talk in code if we're ever going to outsmart these people."

"And how are going to do that?"

"If we decided to meet, it must be in a particular place that only both of us know."

Danny tilted his head up trying to think of a special place where they had privately met in the past. Since he spent most of his time with Blake either at the lab or the research vessel, his clouded mind couldn't come up with a unique place. He momentarily shut off the world around him, hoping his memory would supply him with a clue as to where to go. He'd been best friends with Blake for more than five years, but nothing came to mind.

"This is what I'm thinking. I need you to see Valerie."

Blake's request shocked Danny to his core. It was the last thing he expected Blake to say. Why would Blake want him to see her right when they were teeter-tottering between life and death? Besides, she was the last person he was thinking of at that moment. Four months ago Danny and Valerie had decided to take some time off from each other to figure out how to solve the complicated issues in their past.

"I don't think it's a good idea. It's not even proper," Danny declared through the noisy wind. "She has nothing to do with this."

"I think she is the only one who can help us for now. You have to believe me on this one."

Danny wanted to resist the idea, but since they were running out of options, he decided to put his personal feelings aside to save Elizabeth. He took a deep breath. "What do you want me to do?"

"I hope this will work. I would like you to think of the places that you, me, Valerie and Elizabeth know. It would be very hard for those men tracking us to figure out what we're talking about. It'll all make sense once I text you what I'm planning."

Danny played the scenario in his head. Though Blake's request made sense, he knew that seeing Valerie again would be tough, especially after they had decided to stop dating. Danny was still stuck in the past and felt he was cheating on his former wife, Helen, though she had died more than two years ago. Since Helen was also Valerie's good friend, the claws of guilt affected her, too.

The only way to get Blake's fiancée back was to upload the information on the thumb drive, but the two goons chasing them were making it impossible. If meeting with Valerie to save his best friend's fiancée was necessary, then it had to be done. He reclined in his seat, tilted his head back, and studied the buildings facing the bay to his left. To his right were the dry docks, the massive cranes and U.S. Navy ships moored at the pier being repaired. He could make out the outline of National City. Home to many Filipinos, he had promised Valerie before they separated that he would take her there so she could taste some of his favorite dishes. Deep-fried *Lumpia*; an eggroll for appetizer. Main course would be *Seafood Kare-kare*; a stew with whole shrimps, crabs, squid, mussels topped with eggplants and string beans simmered in a sauce made of toasted ground rice, crushed peanuts. On the side would be a *bibingka*; a sweet rice cake baked in a banana leaf with shredded cheese on top. And for dessert, *Sans Rival*; a cake made with meringue wafers and layered with buttercream and toasted cashews.

The wind blew hard against his face, but not hard enough to strip away the apprehension floating over his head.

The day should have been simple: meet with Blake, upload the data on the thumb drive, and save Elizabeth from the kidnappers. With the situation getting worse with each passing minute, Danny felt he had no other choice.

Danny rested his phone on his lap and looked up. A jet plane was streaking across the clear blue sky and leaving contrail as if slicing the Earth in half. He wondered if he was ready to see her, especially when all hell was breaking loose. As the double-decker bus approached downtown San Diego, Danny looked back at the bridge resembling a piece of stretched taffy. He began to reminisce on when he met Valerie for the first time.

The banquet hall was flooded with guests when Danny arrived alone at a function sponsored by their company. He was wearing a slim-fitting suit with a thin black tie. Shortly thereafter, a woman in a red backless dress arrived, placed her small clutch bag on the table and sat in the chair next to him. She made eye contact with Danny and smiled. He returned her friendly gesture with an even bigger smile, admiring her Latin beauty. She had shoulder-length, dark brown hair and milky white skin. Danny found her smile enchanting, her ha-

zelnut eyes made his heart skip a beat. It was something he hadn't felt in a long time. Since neither one of them knew anyone at the event, and with Blake and Elizabeth accidentally assigned to a different table, they decided to make do with the awkward situation. Danny introduced himself. "I'm one of the scientists who works for the company."

The woman introduced herself as Valerie. He recognized a slight Hispanic accent in her voice.

"I'm one of the architects who helped redesign your new lab."

AS THE NIGHT PROGRESSED, VALERIE wondered just who was this tall, lean muscled man.

She was about to snap another look at Danny when, to her embarrassment, her eyes locked with his. To ease the awkwardness that was building every minute, Danny quickly looked away. Valerie knew in her heart of hearts that she was feeling something different that she hadn't felt with any other man before. The two of them had been together for less than an hour, but the events of the night were already transforming into something she couldn't explain. There was a primordial lust between them brewing in the air. The desire to glide her hands across the muscles rippling in his arms began to burn inside her.

VALERIE WAS DIFFERENT COMPARED TO other women he had met in the past. There was something about this soft-spoken woman. His attraction was multiplying exponentially with each passing minute. It was already too complicated to explain what he was feeling.

He couldn't pull his gaze away from her. The way she looked at him was so intense. She seemed to be interested in everything he said.

Danny knew that there was an attraction brewing beneath the surface. As he spoke to her, he tried to stretch their conversation just so that he could drink in more of the magic of her presence. In return, she rewarded him by adding yet another tidbit of ideas as if she too didn't want the night to end.

When the evening was done, and it was time to go home, Valerie was disappointed to hear that the person who gave her a ride had become sick and had to go home early.

"Blake drove his two-seater sports car," Elizabeth said, her face painted with an expression of feeling sorry. "I could call a taxi."

Not wanting to end the night with her just yet, Danny suggested, "I could take you home. It would be my pleasure, but since it's close to midnight, I have to meet with the marine biology students at the beach. A professor friend of mine asked me to lead a tour of tonight's grunion run."

"What's that?" Valerie asked perplexed.

"They're silvery fish spawning on the sand," Danny replied.

It was already past midnight when Danny and Valerie arrived at the Silver Strand State Beach. The sliver of sandy beach connected the south end of Coronado Island to the southernmost city of Imperial Beach. The students were already huddled together excitedly watching the grunions washing ashore, lit by the full moon hovering up above.

The female grunions were digging their six-inch bodies into the sand with their tails.

"They're laying eggs," Danny commented.

"The other ones curled up next to them are the males?" Valerie asked.

"Yup. They're fertilizing the eggs. Let's say they're mating without physical contact."

"What's the thrill in all of that?" Valerie replied blushing.

THREE

"**WHERE THE FUCK ARE DANNY** and Blake?!" Yuri shouted, turning to Igor.

Igor searched for their whereabouts on the computer monitor in front of him. Just a half hour ago, he knew their exact locations. Blake's cell phone signal was coming in strong from Seaport Village, and Danny's signal was pinging over the Coronado Bridge. But now both of their signatures had dropped off the grid without a trace. Igor scratched his head.

He took his attention away from the laptop. "We've lost them again."

"I don't want to hear this nonsense from you!" Yuri yelled.

"Look, man . . . I was told this was going to be a simple gig when I got the call the other day. These two fuckers are a lot smarter than we thought."

"What do you have?" Yuri snapped.

"Danny, he's on his way to see someone named Valerie."

"Valerie . . . Who is she?"

"I'm already going through his phone record."

Yuri was about to suggest something to Igor when his phone vibrated.

"What the hell is going on?" asked the man at the other end.

"We are resolving the issue right now," Yuri replied, worried that the man who was paying them to catch Danny and Blake might pull them out and send another team to complete the task.

"I'm running out of patience. You and your idiot partner should have resolved this two hours ago," the man said irritably.

"We're hot on the trail. I think we know where Danny is going," Yuri assured the man, ending the call.

Igor was glad to find out that Danny didn't make too many phone calls. Using a unique program that can sort through a person's call log, he transferred Danny's entire incoming and outgoing phone calls in the last six months. An arrogant smile lit up Igor's face while reading the phone numbers Danny frequently called. A particular number with a 619 area code ranked on the top. If not for the hour-long late night calls, he wouldn't have suspected anything different. It was too irresistible for him not to investigate further. He typed the phone number into a website that cross-referenced phone numbers and addresses. The hourglass spun as the computer retrieved the information. A moment later, a name appeared on the screen.

"Bingo! Her name is Valerie Cervantes," Igor said, victory in his voice.

"I need her address," Yuri demanded.

"I just texted it to you, her workplace included. It's a workday. I don't think she'll be home. But wait a minute."

Igor called Valerie's work number. The receptionist picked up. In a professional tone pretending he needed to make a flower delivery, he asked, "Is Valerie Cervantes in?"

The receptionist replied, "Would you like to schedule an appointment? I can help you. She is in, but busy with a client."

He glanced at the clock on the bottom of the computer screen. It was exactly 11 a.m.

"What do you have?" Yuri asked.

"Forget about her house, Danny is on the way to her office as we speak."

Yuri and Igor climbed inside the van and headed straight to the historic Gaslamp Quarter.

FOUR

VALERIE GLANCED AT THE CLOCK hanging on the wall wishing it would go faster. It was fifteen minutes before noon. Her morning had been hectic, seeing high-maintenance clients wanting to redesign their kitchens and bathrooms. She wondered what she would have for lunch. *Panang* curry from the Thai restaurant around the corner? Perhaps the newly opened sushi place two blocks away? Although the extensive international food selections made her mouth water, the thought of eating alone put a crease in her face. She locked her computer screen and dropped her phone in her handbag. As she pushed her office chair away from her desk, she was surprised to find Danny standing at the door, looking right at her. Four months ago, they had decided to stop seeing each other. The issue was simple. Danny had found out that Valerie was Helen's good friend. When he revealed that he was once married to Helen, their heated romance began to thaw from the mutual guilt. They both felt as if they were cheating on Helen, even though she had passed away more than two years ago in a mysterious car accident.

Thinking that Danny had come to his senses and returned to patch things up, Valerie's pupils dilated in excitement. She had anticipated that Danny would tell her that he'd missed her and wanted her back in his life.

Valerie sat frozen behind her desk staring at Danny's lean physique, honed by daily rituals of surfing in the mornings and jogging several nights a week. She was still attracted to Danny's tall, handsome features and his dark chestnut eyes.

She wanted to ask Danny why he had suddenly shown up at her office without even texting or calling. It was uncharacteristic of him.

DANNY WAS QUIET AS HE stared at Valerie. He lost himself in the depths of her eyes with their long, upturned eyelashes. As he stood a few feet away from her, he longed for the days when he could approach her without any hesitation and run his fingers through her dark brown hair. He wanted to pull her tight against his chest and plant his lips on hers, but wondered if it was the appropriate thing to do since they hadn't talked to each other for months. He marveled at her clear-skinned cheeks, gently dusted with a fuchsia blush. It was no wonder Danny couldn't resist her when he met her the first time, he thought. She was still beautiful even in the fluorescent lighting of her office.

Danny approached her, ignoring her pouted lips.

"Are you all right?" Valerie asked. "You seemed distressed."

"It's about Elizabeth," Danny replied, his voice cracking.

"Did something happen to her?"

Danny paused for a moment, not sure how to deliver the bad news.

"She was kidnapped."

The news hit Valerie hard. Her face sagged from the shock as the muscles in her arms weakened. She slumped back in her chair.

"How could this happen? Blake and Elizabeth are getting married in a month! I'm her maid of honor."

"I'm sorry for just showing up to be the bearer of the bad news," Danny muttered apologetically.

"Are you just here to tell me that? What can I do? I'm an architect, not a detective."

"I'm here because . . . I need your help."

"What can I do Danny? I'm not Wonder Woman."

"The kidnappers want me to upload certain data on this thumb drive to a specific IP address as ransom," Danny replied, holding up the thumb drive in his hand.

"What's that got to do with me? Is that all you need? A computer? Use my computer to transfer the data then," Valerie said, standing up from her chair and turning the computer monitor to Danny.

"It's not that simple. The thumb drive can only be read by either the dedicated computer from the lab or from the laptop Blake is carrying."

"Then just go back to the lab and upload it."

"I wish it was that simple, but there are goons waiting for us at the gates. I was just there earlier and almost got nabbed. Every time Blake and I try to rendezvous, these pesky guys show up from out of nowhere. Blake is confident that our phones have been hacked, and that our every move is being monitored."

"This is a police matter."

"No . . . we can't tell the authorities. We were warned not to call any law enforcement agencies or she will be killed. We were given only till tomorrow evening at seven to complete the task."

"And you are here because?"

"I really don't know what Blake is thinking. He instructed me to come see you and to turn on my phone at exactly noon," Danny said, glancing at the clock on the wall.

"That's a minute away."

Danny pressed the power button on his phone. A few seconds later, it vibrated. He placed the phone on the desk and pressed the speaker button.

"Blake, I'm here with Valerie," Danny blurted out.

"Danny told me what had just happened," Valerie added. "I'm so sorry."

"I don't have much time to explain, since the men chasing us are probably listening and are triangulating our coordinates. Valerie, I think you are the only one who can help Danny and me."

"How?"

"I'd like you to go to the place where you first told Elizabeth that you and Danny were dating. She briefly mentioned it to me. Nobody else knows where that is. I hope that we can meet there without any interruptions and upload the data. I'll meet you there in an hour. I'm shutting my phone down now so I can't be tracked. Please do the same on your phones. Talk to you when you get there."

Danny was about to speak when a loud commotion echoed out from the front lobby. Two men were talking with thick eastern European accents. Valerie shot a look at Danny, fear in her eyes. Making sure they weren't walking straight into the attackers from earlier, Danny peeked from behind the doorframe. His fears were confirmed as he spotted his ponytailed assailant with his bald accomplice holding a bouquet of flowers.

CURIOUS AS TO WHAT WAS going on outside, Valerie stuck her head out the door but went too far. Danny pulled her away from the men's line of sight. Her breast pressed against his chest. Heat tingled in her skin while her pulse pounded in her wrist. Beads of sweat slowly rolled down her cheeks. Her nerves began firing, causing her face to flush with a tinge of pink.

She remembered the first time she had the same reaction in his presence. Danny took her by boat for a tour of the San

Diego coastline. While approaching the shore, their boat lost power. Luckily, they were close to the beach. She could see a hang glider soaring up above, its rainbow-colored sail, a dot on the blue sky. Danny jumped in the water and pushed the boat to the beach. Desperately searching for a phone signal, they walked further inland. Little did they realized that they had wandered into the clothing optional Black's Beach.

When Danny gazed back at her, she found herself in kissing distance.

"Are they the men chasing you?" Valerie asked, slightly pulling away from him.

"No doubt. The one with the ponytail almost killed me. We need to get out of here. This place isn't safe anymore. They know who you are."

She put her hand on her lips feeling scared, but she knew Danny very well. He was very independent and resourceful. Knowing that the two men were also after her now, she realized that she had no choice but to help him save the life of their dear friend. And with Danny's black belt in *Arnis*, the martial arts of stick fighting, she was confident that she'd be safe in his presence.

Valerie dropped her phone in her handbag, slung the strap over her shoulder, and urged, "We have to leave now."

"I don't think we can make it past them," Danny protested.

"The back door—I know the way," Valerie said, grabbing his arm.

FIVE

BLAKE PARKED HIS CAR AND shut off the engine. He looked out his window, watching the tourists strolling along the pathways. Checking his watch, he expected Danny and Valerie would be rolling into the half-empty parking lot sometime soon. He got out of his car and rushed over to the statue of Juan Rodriguez Cabrillo that stood proudly overlooking San Diego Bay—one of the first Europeans to arrive in the San Diego Bay back in 1542.

San Diego is the birthplace of California. Cabrillo, after a long voyage from New Spain (presently Mexico), arrived on the shores of San Diego to conquer the new land, to bring Spain glory and with the expectation of discovering gold.

Blake was sure that he was in the right place. The ocean breeze soothed him, but it wasn't enough to calm his nerves. He shifted his gaze to downtown San Diego. Danny and Valerie were somewhere out there in the hustle and bustle of the city. He combed through his memory, gathering each detail Elizabeth had told him. From what he could remember, she had mentioned spending the day with Valerie as a sisterly retreat. It was that day when Valerie mentioned that she was seeing Danny.

Thinking he might be in the wrong spot, Blake hiked up the pathway leading to the Point Loma Lighthouse.

He looked up at the chalky-colored building, its tubular glass casing protruding from its sloped, dark brown roof. He remembered Elizabeth mentioning she was standing on the stairs when Valerie made a passing comment that Danny had just kissed her recently. Blake climbed the stairwell and stood outside the main door, surveying his surroundings. Though he was anxious to be done with their dilemma, he couldn't help but appreciate the smooth features of the ocean below him, sailboats lazily floating by. A large container ship pushed through the water, heading out towards the open sea. Besides the out-of-towners wandering through the pathways, the place was virtually empty. Fearing that the two men chasing him might have already tracked him, he continued to march up the spiral staircase. He passed the dining room, an old cast-iron stove occupying most of the room.

Finally reaching the top, Blake looked down the wooden spiral staircase. The elliptical shape seemed to resemble an eye. He crouched down and peeked outside the window. He traced the line of white picket fences for any sign of either Danny or Valerie, but they were nowhere in sight.

Wondering if maybe he was in the wrong place, he rushed back to his car and drove down to the tide pools. Out the window he could see the new Point Loma Lighthouse, built when the original one was shut down.

Blake walked the uneven cliffs. He looked down at the spaces between the rocks, only to find lovers cuddling. He remembered the four of them sitting in one of the alcoves. Danny had brought out a bottle of almond-flavored champagne from his jacket pocket as Valerie pulled four plastic champagne flutes out of her bag. "It had to be here," Blake thought to himself.

Off in the far distance, a family was looking down on the tide pools as seawater rushed in, filling the cracks. Hoping that Danny and Valerie were hiding in one of the rock formations, he slowly proceeded—careful not to slip and fall—as the moist smell of algae filled his nose.

He overheard two men speaking in a foreign language that sounded eastern European. He crouched down, pretending to be focused on the depressions in the rocks. A tiny crab scuttled away from him. Clumps of barnacles like tiny volcanoes stared at him. He searched his surroundings, digging his knee into the wet rock to lower himself even more, alongside a mauve-colored starfish clinging to the side of the rock. He saw the two men talking, about 20 feet away. He was glad to see it was just a couple of tourists, cameras hanging around their necks.

Breathing a sigh of relief, he checked the time on his wristwatch again. It was 1:00 p.m., exactly an hour since he spoke to Danny and Valerie.

Although Blake didn't want to call Danny, fearing his phone's signal could be tracked, he felt that he didn't have any other choice at this point. Time was running out.

Six

THE GASLAMP QUARTER WAS PACKED when Danny and Valerie walked out onto Fifth Avenue. Though their romantic past still lingered in their minds, Danny and Valerie were all business. The task at hand was too serious to let their emotions get in the way. Elizabeth was suffering more and more with each passing minute; getting her to safety was their top priority. With hurried strides, they wove through the tourists who had just disembarked from the cruise ship docked at the port, walking around fixated on their smartphones, oblivious to their surroundings.

VALERIE TRIED TO KEEP UP with Danny wondering where he would take her next. They turned onto the adjacent street, covered with men in business suits and women in high heels and pencil cut skirts promenading at a leisurely pace. A part of her wanted to tug on his sleeve and ask him why he had suddenly decided to end the magic between them. She thought that he only needed a few days to think about which way their relationship needed to go, but when Danny stopped calling, she blamed herself for ruining what they had going and decided not to bother him anymore. She pushed her query aside, knowing the timing wasn't right. Her best friend's survival depended on them. Resolving their personal issues had to wait. She didn't want to argue with Danny.

DANNY SHOT A GLANCE AT Valerie. Worrying that he might lose her as she struggled to advance, trying not to trip in her high heels on the uneven sidewalk, he slowed down. He remembered that their fingers had been interlaced the last time they had walked this street together. Their pace had been so slow, as if neither of them ever wanted the night to end.

Danny swiveled his head amidst the thickening crowd, checking to see if the men chasing him earlier were in the vicinity. He was relieved to find no one suspicious.

"WEREN'T WE AT SILVER STRAND Beach when you told Elizabeth that we were dating?" Danny queried.

"No, that's not it," Valerie assured him with conviction in her voice.

"Are you sure? We only have one shot to do this right."

Valerie thought of that night when Danny asked her to have dinner with her for the first time.

The restaurants in San Diego's Little Italy had lines snaking out their front entrances with patrons wanting to celebrate their Saturday night when Danny and Valerie arrived. As they walked along India Street, Valerie could see waiters pouring olive oil and balsamic vinegar onto small dishes with warm Italian bread. She was wearing a purple shift dress with a thin scarf around her neck. Danny had on dark blue slacks with a long-sleeved, slim-fitted shirt. Danny talked about his latest research on the ocean. She found it fascinating that the compound he had invented, Rx-18, could one day save the world's oceans from overfishing.

In turn, Danny listened to her talk about the houses she was commissioned to design. Over a glass of white wine and a plate of pasta they talked about their time in college.

"I went to New York for my architecture degree but came back to San Diego after graduation," Valerie said.

He explained that he belonged on the ocean, and that San Diego was the best place to nurture his passion.

It was almost midnight when their first date ended. Danny drove her back to her apartment in Hillcrest, north of downtown.

Like the true gentleman that he was, he opened the car door for her and walked her all the way to her apartment.

When they arrived at the front door, the situation became awkward. Neither one of them knew what to do next.

"I had a good time," Valerie commented.

"I'm glad you did," Danny said, gazing at her eyes.

Danny and Valerie were like two teenagers experiencing their first time alone with the opposite sex. Danny stepped closer to her. Though she knew Danny wasn't the type who hesitated to get what he wanted, she tried to resist his advance and took a step back, but when she banged her ankle on the door, she had nowhere to run. He slowly stroked her hair.

"You're so beautiful," Danny whispered.

With just his mere touch, her hormones shifted into overdrive, sparks flying all the way to the stratosphere. In his presence, she was taken to a higher place. It was nothing she had ever felt before.

She could tell Danny was burning with desire as he stood just inches away from her. She had wondered all night when Danny would finally make the move. As Danny was about to lean in for a kiss, she squeezed her eyes shut, her heart banging in her chest. Not a moment too soon, she felt Danny's warm lips on hers. Their mouths fused together, the ecstasy of his moist kiss took her to the first level of heaven. Her belly flipped inside as a riot of emotions churned. Danny's warm hands began to caress the side of her neck. His touches put her at ease, and her tensed muscles immediately began to relax. She never thought that she would ever experience such pleasure down on earth. As she took him deeper into her mouth, the noise of the passing cars disappeared. Sensations of lightness were all converging at a single point. Danny pulled her tight against his chest. With only a thin piece of fabric separating her bare skin from his, her nipples tingled at the tips, hardening in excitement.

His lips brushed the side of her neck, the smell of vanilla and honey hovering over her skin. Valerie looked up as she sighed in ecstasy. She placed her arms around his shoulders, then gently pulled him closer. His lips glided across the back of her right ear. All that Valerie could do was to look up at the star-filled sky as Danny kissed her in ways she never knew could be so sensual.

After a few minutes of passionate kissing, Danny pulled away from her and just looked at her as if she was going to disappear like a bubble if he took his eyes away from her.

Something about the way he looked at her, told her that he was entering the deepest core of her soul.

CHECKING TO SEE IF THE two men were nearby, Danny stepped into a small space in front of the Old City Hall building. It was hard to believe, but the streets now lined with clothing stores, gelato shops, bars, and restaurants were once occupied with bordellos and gambling halls in the late 1800s.

He approached one of the posts built along the sidewalk with five white globes on top of it, searching for any sign of his assailants. Confident that the coast was clear, he turned to Valerie and said, "Let's stop here for a minute while you try to remember where you met with Elizabeth."

"Let me think," Valerie replied, readjusting her high heels. "That was a Friday. Elizabeth and I had just come back from the Point Loma Lighthouse after hiking for two hours. We were hungry, and Elizabeth was seriously craving Mexican food so we drove down Sports Arena Boulevard but didn't find anywhere we'd like to eat at, so we drove a bit further until we ended up in Old Town. That's it! Old Town—I remember it now. We were sitting at one of the courtyard tables when she flat out asked me if we were seeing each other. I told her that we'd been dating. When I asked her how she knew you, Elizabeth said that you and Helen had gone to the Philippines to rescue Blake from his kidnappers."

"Are you sure?"

"I'm positive. I could still picture my reaction that day. It was such a small world. Helen, Elizabeth, and I were good friends. The three of us had known each other since college."

"Why do you think Blake knows that?"

"She might have mentioned it to Blake. I asked Elizabeth's advice if we were doing the right thing," Valerie lamented.

Danny paused for a moment and tried to process the blame she had just admitted. He thought he was the only one who felt guilty. He wished that the crisis that they were in would be over soon so he could take Valerie to a private place and have a heart-to-heart talk. He needed to know where they stood. Four months of cooling off still hadn't worked. He still found himself waking up in the middle of the night thinking about her.

"We need to get to Old Town right away," Danny said.

SEVEN

WITH THE TWO MEN CHASING them still in the periphery, it was too risky to go back to Horton Plaza where his car was parked. He feared that the two contract killers might already be waiting to ambush them when they arrived. Danny decided that taking the trolley out of downtown to Old Town would give them the best chance of slipping out undetected.

Danny and Valerie were rounding a corner, heading to the Santa Fe Depot trolley station, when to his astonishment, Danny spotted the ponytailed man and his partner already approaching them.

Danny and Valerie had already been seen.

The two men had advanced close enough that they were now in striking distance. Danny was astonished by their resourcefulness. They weren't going to stop until they had the thumb drive or killed Danny. In his periphery, Danny saw a convenience store selling newspapers, gums and chocolate candies and fruits. Knowing neither he nor Valerie could outrun their attackers, Danny pulled down the fruit stand outside. Apples, pears, oranges, grapes, bananas and red plums came tumbling down to the ground.

"We need to go now," Danny directed, grabbing Valerie by the arm and leading her away from the two men.

FOCUSED ON CATCHING DANNY, YURI didn't see the orange rolling in his path. Just as his right foot was about to make contact with the ground, it instead landed on top of the round fruit. His boot crushed it, exposing the pulps and flattening the rind—turning it into a roller skate. His foot slid forward and his momentum threw off his balance. His knee buckled beneath him and he came crashing down on the hard pavement, landing on his right hip. The impact sent pain shooting down his leg as he lay there, unable to get up.

Meanwhile, Igor was running at full speed just a few feet behind Yuri. He didn't have enough time to stop and avoid his companion who was now sprawled face down on the concrete sidewalk. Igor's left foot hooked onto Yuri's armpit, sending him flying face-first into the wooden fruit stand sprawled across the ground.

DANNY AND VALERIE QUICKLY CROSSED the street determined to put a safe distance between them and the two men. Just as he was stepping over the median, Danny heard screeching tires. He grabbed Valerie by the waist to keep her from getting run over. A medium-sized SUV stopped a few inches away from her, almost brushing her thigh. Danny raised his hands apologetically at the stunned driver talking on his cellphone.

Danny shot a quick glance behind him hoping the two men were still tangled up at the fruit stand. Through the thick crowd milling in the streets, he could see the tops of the two men's heads about two blocks away. The blood in his brain drained from fear. He tossed the idea of outrunning the goons, knowing that the two killers were well equipped to capture them. With the situation deteriorating with each passing second, he had to come up with a viable escape plan or neither one of them would make it through the next hour alive. He turned his head to the alley on his right. They could cut across, come out the other side, and blend back in with the pedestrians.

"Quick—over there!" Danny exclaimed, pointing to the passageway that would lead them to safety.

The sour smell of dumpsters overfilled with rotting food and rancid cooking oil filled in the shaded alley. Valerie covered her nose to mask the overwhelming odor.

A cat on the prowl lowered its head and followed Danny and Valerie's footsteps with its sharp, turquoise-colored eyes. Then it began to back away from them. Danny shot a glance at the cat and saw its whiskers pulled back, caution written all over its feline face. He knew something was wrong. Wanting to know the ominous message the cat was telling him, he turned around and scanned the area for trouble.

His search was quickly over when he saw the Baldy standing at the end of the alleyway with a menacing grin. The hairs along his spine stood up as the threat of being captured became evident. The wildness in the man's eyes suggested that he wanted to kill Danny and finish his pursuit.

But Danny was not going to have any of that. He was determined to defend Valerie and meet up with Blake. That was his intent. If he had to kill the bald man wanting to do him harm, then so be it.

In a fighting stance, Danny curled his fists. Valerie tapped him on the shoulder.

"We're almost out of the alley, run!" Valerie yelled.

Wanting to save their skin from being filleted, Danny and Valerie fled to the other side of the street to escape.

Their hearts sank when they discovered a chain-link fence in the middle of the alleyway. Danny pivoted to see how much time they had. A chill slapped the back of Danny's neck as he realized that the man was sprinting at them, just five arm's lengths away. Fearing that Igor might pull a gun on them, Danny raced directly towards the man.

DANNY'S COURAGEOUS MOVE TOOK IGOR by surprise. Danny galloped towards him with lightning speed. Igor reached for the pistol holstered in his waistband and took aim. Danny swiped it out of his hands. The pistol flew through the air and tumbled near the gutter.

Capitalizing on the momentum, Danny lowered his head like a battering ram and smashed it into Igor's stomach. He could tell that pain cracked through Igor's ribs from the distressed expression on his face. He fell to his knees, gasping for air.

Danny widened his stance and balled his fist. He slammed it directly into Igor's bony cheek. Bright crimson blood oozed out of Igor's face. Danny swung again, this time connecting with Igor's temple, jarring his skull. The force of his punch sent Igor into a disoriented tailspin, causing the bald man to lose his balance and crash into the row of trashcans lining the wall.

Wanting to put him out of commission so he wouldn't be followed anymore, Danny approached Igor again.

The bald man kicked up. The tip of his black boot connected with Danny's inner thigh. A surge of pain shot up his groin. He fell to the ground. The man jumped on top of him and began peppering Danny in the face with nonstop blows. Danny's vision began to spin. He could smell the fruity stench of vodka spewing out of the man's filthy mouth. Danny put his arms in front of him to block the barrage of punches, wanting to protect his face from turning into a punching bag.

NOT WANTING TO STAND ON the sidelines and do nothing, Valerie picked up an empty beer bottle next to her, raised it over her head, and smashed it directly into the back of the Baldy's head.

The amber bottle shattered instantly, shards of glass falling on the pavement.

The man grabbed the top of his head in agony. Using this sliver of opportunity, Danny bent his arm and in an upward motion drilled the tip of his elbow directly into the man's chest. Immediately, the man doubled over in pain, clasping his chest and turning to his side struggling to fill his lungs with much-needed air.

Igor was momentarily disabled.

"Who are these people?" Valerie asked.

"I really don't know. They have been chasing me and Blake all morning. Quick, I'll help you over the fence."

Valerie took off her high heels and planted her foot onto Danny's interlaced hands. She looked deep into his earthy brown eyes for confidence. Placing one hand on the fence and the other on his shoulder for balance, the tips of her hair brushed across Danny's cheeks. He remembered the last time they were this close, both naked and exploring each other's bodies.

He gazed into her hazel brown eyes flecked around the edges with deep citron olive. It felt like he was peeking directly into her soul once again, lost in her being. If it wasn't for the imminent threat of death, Danny would have pressed her back against the red brick wall, tore her clothes off, and made love to her right then and there.

Valerie hesitated for a moment just as she was about to press her full weight into his hands. She had a look of doubt about whether or not she could do it. His voice reassuring her that everything would be OK, Danny said, "Put your other foot on the bar, you can do this."

Trusting him with all her heart, she clawed her fingers through the fence and began climbing. Danny placed one hand on her torso, the other one on her thigh, and pushed her up. She clamped her hand on the top of the fence. Using all of her remaining strength, she climbed over the barrier, hit the ground, then steadied herself to replace her shoes.

Danny had just jumped over the fence when he heard shouts coming from the alleyway. The man with the ponytail was running towards them at full speed. Danny couldn't understand what Ponytail was saying, but from the gist of it he was shouting at the bald man that Danny had just clobbered into oblivion.

With the fence behind them and Yuri charging at them from ahead, Danny and Valerie were caught between a rock and a hard place.

Panic struck them further when the Igor began to stand up. They were trapped. Either one of the two men could shoot them anytime. With the situation getting worse with each passing second, Danny searched for another way out.

"We have nowhere to run," Valerie lamented.

Just then, he looked up and noticed a low-hanging fire escape ladder.

Danny jumped up and tried to grab it. The tips of his fingers barely touched the ladder. He wasn't able to pull it down.

"It's too high!" Danny yelled with frustration.

Trying to solve the deteriorating situation they were embroiled in, he picked up an empty trashcan. He set it up at the base of the ladder and used it for extra height. Danny bent his legs and, with all the strength he had, jumped up. His hand connected to the bottom of the ladder. The round steel felt good in his hands. A moment later, he was able to pull it down.

Danny looked behind him. Yuri was getting closer by the second as he sprinted towards them.

"Hurry, we need to climb up!" Danny said, waving Valerie to get closer.

Valerie pleaded, "I'm scared, Danny!"

Trying to subside her fears, Danny pulled her close to him. He planted a kiss on her forehead and whispered in her ear, "We can do this. We have to."

He wrapped his arms around her slender waist and lifted her up. Valerie reached for her high heels and slipped them off her feet once more. She sprang up towards the end of the ladder.

Barefoot and holding her high heels, Valerie climbed up the ladder.

"Why don't you just drop your shoes and forget about it," Danny yelled as he followed her up.

"I don't want to get a cut from a nail or broken glass!" Valerie fired back. "Do you know how hard it is to walk barefoot?!"

"Walking on those heels looks more difficult," Danny countered.

Her foot slipped off one of the steps. Danny quickly reacted and pressed his hand on her buttocks. As she took a step up, Danny followed.

Finally reaching the landing, Valerie turned to Danny and said, "I'm fine now. You can take your hand off my butt."

"Oh . . ." Danny reacted embarrassingly, taking his hand off her rear.

Wanting to make sure that they couldn't be followed, Danny pulled the ladder up so the two men chasing them could not catch up.

Fright puffed in his face as soon as Danny realized that the door leading inside the building was locked.

"Damn!" he cursed under his breath.

"Use that," Valerie suggested, pointing to a potted plant.

With both hands, Danny raised the potted plant over his head and smashed it into the doorknob. The handle broke free from the door.

"Stand back!" Danny warned.

With his leg strength, he kicked the door. It flew open.

Just as he was about to enter the door, he looked down. The two men were already running to the building's front entrance.

Danny quickly realized his big mistake. The hundred-year-old structure they had just walked into could either be their salvation or their death trap.

It was hard to see in the darkened hallway, lit only by a few dying light bulbs along the walls.

Danny had to think real fast about what he should do next. He thought of going down the stairs and fleeing through the back door, but with the two men already near the building, that was out of the question. There was no other escape but to go further up.

"I don't think we can outrun them. Let's head to the roof," Danny said, already sprinting up the stairs.

As they ascended the wide stairs, Valerie turned to Danny. "Maybe we could hide in one of the rooms?"

"But we don't know who is in these rooms. We could be facing the end of a shotgun if we just barge in unannounced."

Although Valerie's idea made sense, even if they found an empty room, the two men would surely inspect each room and wouldn't leave the building until they had been found.

Reaching the rooftop was their only option.

The San Diego skyline was beautiful under the canopy of the topaz sky. The swelling clouds reflecting the bright midday light blinded Danny and Valerie as soon as they reached the building's rooftop. Danny squinted, searching for something he could devise as a weapon. The beige rooftop was barren, besides a couple of weathered lawn chairs.

"Shit!" Danny yelled. "We're trapped!"

It would only be a matter of minutes before Yuri and Igor would be on top of the roof to capture them. He pushed the thought aside. Danny knew that he'd be powerless to defend himself and Valerie against the two thugs carrying guns.

Danny wished he could carry Valerie in his arms, jump off the building in a leap of faith, and fly over the streets like a superhero onto the safety of the other buildings. But he was just an ordinary man with no special powers. Relying on his wits was his only option.

Wanting to know the progress of the two thugs, he skittered to the building's edge. The view of the street below from five stories up was dizzying. To his dismay, Yuri and Igor were at the front entrance, pounding on the door.

"They'll be here soon," he said, backing away from the wall.

Yuri slammed his foot into the door near the lock but it wouldn't budge. Frustrated, he summoned Igor. With the same determination, Igor also kicked the door, but to no avail.

"Back off!" Yuri warned, pushing Igor away from the door.

Yuri unzipped his knapsack and retrieved a small clay explosive. He formed the malleable substance around the lock and attached the triggering mechanism.

After setting the timer to five seconds, Yuri backed away from the door. The charge exploded, blowing the door wide open.

Guns drawn, sweeping from side-to-side, Yuri and Igor entered the building ready to shoot anyone perceived as a threat.

Desperate, Danny searched the sides of the building for a fire escape ladder hoping they could use it to climb back down. Unfortunately, the ladder only reached the top floor and not all the way to the roof. It was at least a fifteen-foot jump. Jumping down was out of the question. One of them would surely break an ankle, possibly a leg, if they attempted the daring move. While looking for something they could use to climb down, he saw a coiled rope and an aluminum ladder along the raised edge of the building.

He picked up the ladder, expanded it, and raised it upright. Using all his upper arm strength, he walked the ladder to the edge of the building.

"What are you doing?" Valerie asked with a perplexed voice.

"Stay back."

Eyeing the adjacent building, he tipped the ladder over. It made a loud crunching sound when the other end of the ladder hit the rooftop across the alley.

They now had a makeshift bridge.

"We're going to walk on the ladder to get to there," Danny said, pointing to the building next to them.

"You gotta be kidding me!" Valerie exclaimed, her eyes widening in disbelief. "I don't think I can do it . . . I have a fear of heights!"

"We have no other choice. We can do this. I'm just as scared as you are," Danny reassured her, reaching for her hands.

"Are you sure about this?" Valerie asked. "I need you to walk across with me. I don't think I can do it alone."

"We can't walk together. The two of us on the ladder at the same time will be too heavy. The ladder might fold and collapse," Danny responded, wrapping the rope around Valerie's waist. "If you fall, this will save you."

Danny began to second-guess his plan. Maybe jumping down to the fire escape ladder on the first landing was a better idea. Potentially breaking a leg wasn't a bad option compared to falling down to their deaths. Just then, they heard a loud banging coming from the door he had just locked behind him. Even if he wanted to ditch the ladder idea, it was now too late. He had no choice but to go ahead with his plan.

"We need to go now!" Danny shouted.

REALIZING THAT THEY HAD RUN out of alternatives for escape, Valerie took her high heels off again and stuffed them in her handbag. Firmly placing her hands on the steps, her bare feet planted on the sides of the ladder, she began to crawl forward. She looked down at the alley, the dizzying height enough to make her cringe. When she reached the midpoint, the ladder started to bend downward and wobble uncontrollably. Her fear of falling was paralyzing.

"Oh my god, Danny, I'm gonna fall!" Valerie shouted.

"I'm holding the ladder steady. You're going to be fine. The rope is your safety. Keep going. You're almost there!" Danny shouted.

Valerie took her eyes off the ground below and steadied her sights on the building ahead of her. One step at a time, she put one foot forward, then the other.

As soon as she set foot on the rooftop, her heart beating faster than the speed of sound, she calmed down. She turned around to signal Danny that she was fine and that he could cross right away. Just as she was about to wave her hand, she saw the chair propped against the doorknob inching forward.

"Danny! They're behind you!"

Danny glanced over his shoulder. The door was already opening.

"Hold the ladder down!" Danny shouted.

Valerie gripped the ladder and pressed her knees down on one of the steps.

THE LAST THING HE WANTED was to get into a fight with the two men. He was certain that he wasn't going to win. And if either one of them got ahold of the ladder, all they had to do was to push it off and he'd drop like a rock and plunge to his death. Having no more time to stall, he quickly advanced forward.

Danny was about a few feet from reaching the edge of the building when he noticed alarm in Valerie's face. Her panicked expression said it all.

"Hurry . . . they're coming!"

Not wishing to find out what fate awaited him, he tripled his efforts.

Danny quickly glanced behind him. Yuri and Igor were already reaching for the ladder. He focused on what was ahead of him. He only had ten more feet to reach safety. On his hands and knees at least fifty feet up in the air on an aluminum ladder that was about to be shaken loose, Danny did the unthinkable. He got up and started running. The soles of his shoes made contact with the ladder's steps, the frame bending as he pressed his weight. With one misstep, his foot could slide off and he could fall to his death. But he didn't have time to play it safe.

Just a few feet away, he felt the ladder lift behind him. He looked back. What he saw shot fear though the base of his skull. They had raised the ladder and were pulling it back so that it would fall, taking Danny with it. The ladder started to incline downward. He placed his feet flat on the sides of the ladder. Carefully balancing, he let go of the ladder. Gravity did the rest and he began sliding forward.

Suddenly, the ladder gave way. He reached for the edge of the roof, but couldn't grasp it to save his live.

His ultimate fear was happening. He was going to fall.

Just then, he felt the rough edges of the rope in his hand. He gripped it tight, holding on for dear life.

He smashed into the side of the building. The rope began shearing his palms. His hands felt like they were on fire, and he couldn't hang on any longer. His grasp slackened and he began descending.

Then there was a miracle.

His plummet to the ground was interrupted when his hand made contact with a large knot on the rope. He was saved from his nosedive, but still dangling between the earth and sky.

Immediately, he felt around with his feet for a window frame or a crack in the wall so he could climb up. But the wall was smooth and his situation hopeless.

He was about to give up when the rope suddenly stiffened. He was ascending inch by inch.

Valerie was pulling him up.

As soon as he reached the edge of the rooftop, he threw his legs over. With quick thinking, Valerie reached over and grabbed him by the belt. She pulled him up to safety.

"You OK?" Valerie asked anxiously.

"I banged my hip but I'm all right. Thank you."

"Thank me later. We need to get off this building," Valerie replied, helping him up. "We need to go now. I just saw them go back down," she pointed out.

BUILT IN 1915 TO RECEIVE the influx of passengers attending the Panama-California Exposition, the sight of Santa Fe Depot was a relief when Danny and Valerie saw it as they raced through West Broadway. The long, beige Spanish Colonial Revival-style structure with its two bell towers gilded with yellow and blue tile—the turn-of-the-century design was dwarfed by the surrounding buildings.

They walked inside looking for the ticket machine so they could get to Old Town. Inside, the hall was lined with long benches filled with passengers waiting for their train to arrive. As they walked across the polished floor, Valerie studied the chandeliers hanging from the vaulted ceiling. She had been through the station many times but was still in awe with its architectural design.

"I think we're in the wrong place. Isn't this for trains heading north towards Los Angeles? We need to get to the trolley," Danny said.

"I think you're right."

Realizing they were in the wrong spot, Danny and Valerie wasted no time exiting the building, crossing the tracks, and making their way to the America Plaza trolley station.

They stood in front of the ticket machine, slightly intimidated because neither of them had been on the trolley for a long time. It would have been simpler to skip buying tickets and get on the trolley, as the two men could arrive at any time. But if they got onboard without a ticket, the risk of getting caught by the trolley inspector would not only result in fines, but attracting too much attention could be deadly.

Danny inserted a bill. The machine spat out two one-way tickets.

Though the station's high-arched metal roof was stylish, Danny and Valerie couldn't appreciate its grandiosity as they nervously waited for the trolley to arrive.

The crossing sound rang, red lights flashed, and the barricade came down blocking vehicle traffic from both sides. From a distance, Danny could see the bright red trolley snaking into the station. Danny and Valerie edged closer to the yellow marking on the edge of the platform and anxiously waited for the trolley to stop.

The doors hissed open and a tidal wave of people going about their ordinary day streamed from the trolley car. Following the other passengers boarding the trolley, they slid inside a half-empty car, glad to find two empty seats. They rested their tired bodies from the stress of running nonstop. Danny looked through the window. He was glad to see that neither of the two goons was around.

The doors closed and the trolley's horn made two quick bursts. The electric motors steadily hummed and the metal wheels clicked onto the rails as they pulled away from downtown San Diego.

Danny shot a glance at their fellow passengers, standing in the aisle trying not to fall as the trolley swayed from side to side. He wished for the day to be over, the data uploaded and everything else faded into memory.

Valerie rested her head on Danny's shoulder, her hands trembling in apprehension as she tried to grasp the gravity of their situation. Danny noticed that her eyes were dripping with tears. He pulled her tight against his chest to comfort her.

"I'm sorry for getting you involved in this mess," he said as he smoothed her tense back muscles with his palm.

Valerie didn't respond. Instead, she looked out the window, watching the tall condominiums smearing in the background. He could tell that her racing heart was beginning to calm with his arm draped around her.

A few minutes later, she muttered, "It's OK. We need to get Elizabeth back."

Danny slouched in his seat and reviewed the trolley map, the routes connected like arteries leading to the heart, hoping they'd arrive just in time to meet with Blake.

EIGHT

FOR AN ORDINARY FRIDAY MORNING, Old Town San Diego was unusually busy with sightseers. It was in this spot where the Spanish chose to settle for good.

Danny and Valerie passed by a group of elementary school students on a school excursion, all wearing lime green T-shirts with their school logo printed on the front.

"Are you sure this is the right place?" Danny asked.

"I think so," Valerie said as they walked inside the courtyard of the Casa de Estudillo—one of the original houses built in Old Town.

Valerie hesitated for a moment, unsure if she was in the right place. She moved closer to a small fountain. The sound of water splashing against the stones was soothing, but it wasn't enough to calm her worried mind.

"Looks like no one is here."

Valerie closed her eyes for a moment as she tried to rummage through her cluttered memory.

"We were at a restaurant when I told her about us. That's it," Valerie declared as she exited through the main entrance under the bell tower.

When they entered the courtyard, Danny expected Blake to jump out of the bushes. To his left was a stage. Young women in traditional Mexican dresses and young men with matching coats and wide-brimmed hats were performing a Mexican folk dance. The women tossed their wide skirts left and right, bending back and forth with graceful steps. The men were stomping and kicking their pointed boots on the wooden stage, their hands tucked behind their backs.

"I'm pretty sure this is where Elizabeth and I were together that day," Valerie hinted.

"Which restaurant?"

Valerie paused for a moment. She was absolutely certain that it was in an Old Town restaurant when she first told Elizabeth about them. She could vividly remember having a margarita at midday.

"I don't think it's here," Valerie snapped, remembering she had just led Danny to the wrong place. "It's the one across the way."

A GREETER WAS STANDING BEHIND the podium in a traditional Mexican dress—red at the top, green in the middle, and white on the oversized skirt. She welcomed them with a wide smile. Valerie spoke in Spanish asking her if they could be seated at the table near the pink bougainvillea.

"That's the same table we sat at," Valerie pointed out to Danny.

THE PLACE WAS BUSY. EXCITED conversations hung in the air. Patrons sat at the table next to them, clad in office attire, drinks in their hands.

A few minutes later, the waitress arrived and carefully placed a wide-rimmed margarita glass in front of Valerie, crystal salts sparkling around the edge. She went around the table and gave Danny the mojito he had ordered. He picked up his tall drink and stared at the large chunks of ice, the sprig of mint, and the thin slices of lime floating inside the glass. He took a sip. The tangy taste of lime, sugar and rum helped calm his racing pulse.

Danny checked the time on his wristwatch. They still had about half an hour to kill before 1:00 pm—when he would be turning his phone back on to answer another call from Blake. All they could do for now was to sit at their table and bear the awkward feeling of seeing each other again so unexpectedly.

A mariachi band approached them and began singing a Spanish love song. The guitarist strummed his instrument with intensity; its rhythmic pulse reverberating throughout the busy dining hall. The violinist pushed and pulled his bow with slow, controlled movements. Though Danny wasn't fluent in Spanish, he recognized some of the words from the singer. It was something like, "If you can only open your eyes, I'm right here in front of you."

Danny wanted to reach across the table and caress her rosy cheeks like he had done hundreds of times in the past. He wanted to hold her hand so that their beating hearts could be connected once more. Maybe the song being sung was correct. The one he was looking for was right in front of him. Valerie was one of a kind. Letting her slip through his fingers again would be a foolish mistake.

The mariachi gathered closer around their table. The bass guitar player was wearing a ruffled shirt inside a black overcoat, his pants dotted with stars. He started plucking the fat strings of his bass guitar passionately, thumping low beats on his chest.

Danny fixed his gaze at Valerie. He was hoping to have forgotten about her during their brief separation, but as he now sat inches away from her, he wondered if it was possible. Why couldn't he forget about Helen and love Valerie without restrictions? He wanted to let his guilt wash away, but he just didn't know how. The lonely nights spent in his apartment were too much to bear. There must be a way to forgive himself and freely love another woman—this woman—again.

A few months after they had started dating, guilt began to grow between Danny and Valerie. Whenever Helen entered their conversation, no matter how romantic things were at the time, the heat of the moment always came to a screeching halt. Just the mere mention of her name caused uneasiness between them.

As he was driving away from Valerie's house one night after a date, images of Helen flashed in his mind. He wondered if falling in love with another woman was like cheating on her though she was already long dead. It shouldn't be. It was unfair to feel that way. He was overreacting. He wondered if he was the one who died, would he forgive Helen if she fell in love again with another man? Would he appear in her sleep and talk to her in her dreams?

Danny had explained the shame pressing on his chest to Valerie—and the torment he was going through. Their situation had become difficult. A few weeks later, Danny decided to stop calling Valerie. Danny was relieved when Valerie didn't bother him with texts and phone calls as he figured out what to do next.

AS VALERIE TOOK A SIP from her margarita glass, heat rose behind her neck. She caught Danny staring at her almost in a daze. His fixation on her sent her heart banging against her chest as if it was about to burst out through her throat. She longed for his touch and wished Danny would find the courage to reach across the table and hold her hands.

She wanted to feel his gentle palms on her soft skin the way she had before. He wouldn't have to say anything. His fingers interlaced with hers would be enough to declare he wanted her too.

As she stole a glance at Danny, she was overwhelmed with longing.

Valerie wondered how their love affair began and how Danny wiggled his way into her heart when love was the last thing she was looking for. Being content by herself disintegrated the minute Danny walked into her life, as if her entire being was suddenly rearranged.

It had all come to a surprise to her when she learned that the man she was attracted to was also the man who had been married to her dear friend. Love came knocking at her heart when she least expected it—barging in in the middle of the night—its annoying calls from the darkened street were too hard to ignore. The only way to stop its scandalous cries was to unlock the front door of her soul and let it in with open arms, silencing the shouts with her embrace.

Being so intimate so soon wasn't the right way to go about things. A hasty move might derail their already fragile meeting.

Wrenching pain stabbed her heart when he disappeared from her life. It was too much to bear. He was her drug of choice at the time when she didn't realize she needed one. Danny was the one in her medicine cabinet to quench the ache in her heart.

Valerie realized that all that needed to be said had already been said. The silence between them was enough to let her know that Danny desired her too.

At that moment, there wasn't much she could do but to drag her gaze away from him. She wished that she could just look at Danny unrestrictedly the way she had always done, completely free from any guilt, before the truth came clawing out from the past. She wanted there to be no secrets between them anymore.

She shot a glance at Danny only to find out that his gaze was already resting on hers. The sudden eye contact was a bit embarrassing. Checking each other out on the pretense of taking it slowly. To keep doing what they had agreed to do. Not to see each other. Some much needed breathing room while they could figure out if they truly belonged to each other. She quickly looked away from him and pretended as if he was just part of the table decorations like the long-stemmed carnation in the tall vase in front of them.

Words were not necessary. The only thing left to do was to follow the desire she felt and to be with him as soon as their ordeal was over.

AT EXACTLY 1:00 P.M., DANNY turned his phone on.

A text message from Blake was already waiting on the locked screen. "Where are you? I've been waiting here more than ten minutes!"

"Read this," Danny said, showing the message to Valerie. "There must be something wrong. I'm sure this is the place."

"We're here at the restaurant," Danny texted.

"What restaurant? That's not where Valerie told Elizabeth about your past. It's at the historical place where San Diego was founded. You know what I mean?"

Danny pondered on what Blake had just told him. He thought he was in the right place, but could be mistaken.

"We're right here where San Diego was first settled," Danny replied. "I'm sure we're in the right place."

"We might be getting the two places confused," Blake said.

"Give us about twenty minutes and we'll be there right away," Danny responded.

He shut his phone and slid it back into his front pocket. Frustrated about the time wasted waiting in the wrong place, he said, "Blake is thinking of a different place. I know where it is now."

THE PRESIDIO OF SAN DIEGO with its bleach-white adobe walls of grand, mission-style architecture overlooked the sprawling Mission Valley. Inside was a museum.

Though it no longer exists, the original Fort Presidio was established as the first European settlement in San Diego in the same area. The fortified living area for settlers, soldiers and missionaries was designed to protect them from any attacks launched by the Native Americans. Within its walls, the colonization of California by the Spanish had begun.

Danny and Valerie climbed the wide staircase.

"He should already be here," Danny said.

"Are you sure this is the place?" Valerie asked.

"It has to be. It's one of the few places built when San Diego was first founded. Let's see if he's inside."

They walked inside the museum, named after Father Junípero Serra who was a saint to many and a villain to more.

The tools of Native Americans were displayed alongside one of the cannons that the Spanish used to control them.

Valerie was shocked to see that the place was empty.

"Let's snoop around the back," Danny said.

They searched for Blake's whereabouts. Doubling their pace, they passed by flowers blooming along the pathway. They ended up on a hill with picnic tables and tall pine trees. Worried that something had gone wrong, Danny turned his phone on. Pressed for time, he didn't even bother texting. Instead, he pressed Blake's number on his speed dial.

"Where are you?"

"I'm here," Blake responded, his voice frantic.

"Are you sure we're talking about the same place?" Danny asked, anxiety in his voice.

"This is getting complicated. I was hoping that my plan to meet by sending cryptic messages was going to be simple, but apparently, it's not working. We can't afford to slip up," Blake said, sounding worried.

"So, what now?"

"We need to go silent to confuse those men chasing us. Don't tell me where you are and turn your phone off right away. Go to a safe place until I figure out our next move. I'll text you in two hours."

"Wait . . . Stay put. I think I know where you are. I'll be there in less than half hour. If I don't show up in time, we'll talk in two hours as planned."

After switching the phone off, Danny turned to Valerie. "We're not safe here anymore. We need to get out of here now."

"Why do you think those two men are chasing us?" Valerie asked as she tried to keep up with Danny's quick steps down the stairs.

"I think those two guys are nothing but paid killers. The same thing happened to Helen and me when we were in the Philippines. Somebody is financing them and calling the shots."

"What's on the thumb drive?"

"Nothing but scientific information, data on fish migration patterns. Why it's important enough to get Elizabeth kidnapped and for those two to want us dead, it puzzles the hell out of me," Danny responded.

"There has to be more to this," Valerie replied, sounding unconvinced.

"About two days ago, the data was deleted from our server. Our IT department tried to figure out what had happened, but no one had any clue. The signal from the deletion came from a remote location."

"No backups?"

"Only on this thumb drive."

"Isn't it strange for a company that size not to have protocols for situations like this?"

"The company specifically designed our network so that no one person can transfer the data. At least two researchers have to be logged in to make changes. Copies can't be made. The system is designed so that the compiled and analyzed data can't be easily shared between scientists. It is proprietary information and anyone who reads it is monitored and recorded."

"Did you see anything *fishy* when you last reviewed it?"

"No. I checked it two days ago, and the prized tunas and other species were moving in the right direction."

"It has to be more than just fish data."

"A day before the data was deleted, a memo was sent out that someone from outside our network had kept trying to log on. As a precaution, Blake and I made a backup copy of the data of the migration pattern so it would be safe. We didn't think much about it till Elizabeth was abducted and we learned about the ransom."

"This whole thing does not make any sense. Even if the kidnappers or the people after you get ahold of the thumb drive, you could always make another copy."

"The thumb drive has a read-only feature and can only be accessed through dedicated hardware or a laptop with a dedicated authenticator. The kidnappers know that, and that's why we're being told to upload the information to their server," Danny replied.

"There must be something on that thumb drive so important that someone would be willing to kill for it."

Danny pondered her comment. Why would anyone go so out of their way to get such information?

"Unless it contains raw data that might mean a whole lot for someone," Danny said.

"Do you have someone you trust who has one of the dedicated computers that can read what's on the thumb drive? And maybe help you upload it?"

Danny was surprised with Valerie's analytical thinking. In his mind fogged with confusion, rushing to get the data uploaded to get Elizabeth back, he hadn't thought of that. The only way to stop the two men from killing them and to get Elizabeth back was to upload the data right away.

"There's only one person that I can think of whose company is actively involved with tracking fish migration."

"A researcher?"

"Yes . . . Dr. Adamson. We need to see him right away."

"Does he know about all this?"

"He has a dedicated laptop that can read what's on the thumb drive and he might even help me upload the data. He also heads a company monitoring fish migration patterns in the north Pacific Ocean. If he can't help us, he should at least be able to lead us to the right people who can help me upload the data."

"That's great," Valerie said.

"I think we can end this soon."

"And the men chasing us?"

"I don't care about those two. If Blake and I upload the information by 7:00 p.m. tomorrow, Elizabeth will be freed. They'll back off. It would be pointless to chase us."

"Where's Dr. Adamson?"

"He's holding a fundraising event in his La Jolla mansion tonight. We can go there this afternoon."

"Without an invitation?" Valerie asked.

"Don't worry about that. We'll sneak in. As long as we're dressed formally, I don't think any of the staffers will notice. His mansion is big."

"But we can't go home and change. We're already being watched."

"We can just go buy new outfits," Danny suggested.

"We can't use our credit cards. As soon as we swipe our cards, we'll be discovered."

Valerie was right. Picking out both a business suit and a beautiful dress could take at least an hour—more than ample time to be discovered by the two men tracking them.

"Or maybe . . . we can go to the bridal shop that Elizabeth had picked out. She took me and her bridesmaids there to get fitted with gowns," Valerie said, her eyes beaming with delight. "Isn't that the same place you're supposed to pick up your tuxedo?"

"Where's the store?"

"Fashion Valley," Valerie replied, already sounding victorious.

Danny searched his surroundings, hoping to get a ride from one of the dozen cars in the parking lot. He found a car with its windows rolled down, a couple of teenagers sitting inside texting. He thought of giving them fifty bucks for a ride.

"I think I might have a plan," Danny said.

Just as they were approaching the car, a taxi stopped behind it. Four people began to step out.

"A taxi would be better," Valerie pointed out.

He walked up to the driver.

"Can we hire you?" Danny asked.

The wavy-haired, dark-skinned driver replied in a thick Indian accent, "I'm sorry very much sir but I have another call."

Danny reached through the window and offered his hand for a handshake. The driver took his hand, a fifty-dollar bill tucked in his palm.

"Let me sweeten the deal. You just have to take us to the Mission San Diego de Alcalá. It shouldn't be more than a fifteen-minute ride. What do you say?"

The driver craned his neck and shot a glance at the passengers he'd just dropped off, busy posing for pictures in front of the building.

"It would be a great very much pleasure sir. Hop in," the driver replied, stuffing the bill in his shirt pocket.

"What's your name?" Danny asked, climbing into the taxi.

"Pradeep," the driver replied, shifting the gear into reverse.

FOUNDED BY JUNÍPERO SERRA DURING the summer of 1769, Mission San Diego de Alcalá was the first church of the chain of 21 missions that were built by the Franciscan friars that ran all the way to Northern California. The friars brought religion with them and the latest know-how at the time in agriculture, but unfortunately, also diseases that would kill a lot of the Native Americans.

Pradeep parked the taxi directly in front of the church.

"Give us a few minutes and we'll be right back," Danny said, exiting the taxi.

The thick brown door swung open when Danny pushed it. The church had several people sitting on the benches, but otherwise was empty. Above, he could hear the choir practicing their choral music. From his periphery, he noticed the flickering candles to his right.

"Come, let's check the pews," Valerie said, leading the search.

Danny checked the parishioners to their left and right hoping Blake would be there. He was disappointed that his best friend wasn't present.

Going out the side door, Danny and Valerie searched the courtyard—walking through the brown tiled pathways lined with flowers and shrubs. After passing by the statue of Junípero Serra, he set his sights on the large bell tower. Again, the place was empty.

Finding Blake looked bleak.

"He's not here," Danny said with the pang of disillusionment in his voice.

NINE

AS THE TAXI SPED TO their destination, Danny stared out the window trying to quell the anxiousness forming in his stomach. It was about 3 p.m. The people in their cars looked relaxed as their day was winding down. Most were probably going home after a long day's work, and perhaps some were on their way to spend some time with friends at restaurants in Mission Valley.

As he observed the hubbub in the heart of the county, he couldn't help but think that California became part of Mexico when it declared its independence from Spain.

Eventually, with the arrival of the trappers, hunters and adventurers, the sleepy state was inundated with settlers. The inevitable happened; The Mexican-American War. The Louisiana Territory had just been purchased from France. With thousands more coming from all over the world during the Gold Rush, California became the 31st state in 1850. California was once a mythical land, now it was a real place. Thus, the vision of America's founders of a nation that began from the Atlantic all the way to the Pacific Ocean became a reality.

Danny wished he could have an ordinary, worry-free day just like those people, without the weight of someone's life on his shoulders. Just a few days ago, he was living like anybody else in the county—running errands and minding his own business. As the taxi steadily flowed along with the other cars on the freeway, he knew that today was no ordinary day. And by the end of day, things could get ugly.

Along the banks of the San Diego River, Fashion Valley Mall's pearl-white buildings appeared from behind the trees through his window. The taxi driver tapped on his brakes as he merged onto the onramp. The lines of cars heading to the mall were long. With the silence in the taxicab growing unbearable, the driver flicked on the radio and the local news boomed through the speakers: There was an accident at the Interstate 5 and 805 merge in the northern part of the county . . . The price of gas went up by five cents . . . Sunrise will be at 6:10 a.m. and sunset at 7:45 p.m . . . Santa Anas—the dry hot winds coming from the desert—some saying the name was derived from the word Santanás or the devil wind—were forecast for the following day. Then, as if it was an afterthought, the reporter commented on the day's surf report. Swells would be 3-5 feet, from waist to head. Danny wished he was on the waves, balancing on his tri-fin surfboard.

Pradeep popped a CD in the stereo and played some Bollywood music. The upbeat tempo lightened the mood.

He turned to Valerie and said something in rapid Hindi. Valerie looked puzzled.

"Sorry, but she's not Indian. She's Mexican," Danny interrupted.

"So . . . so sorry," the driver said. "Forgive my quick assumption."

"You were telling me something?" Valerie asked.

"It's the thought of mine you were a Bollywood movie actress visiting the States."

"You gotta be kidding me?" Valerie blushed.

Danny turned to her and said, "I think our friend Pradeep here is milking us for more tips."

"No, sir, that you're mistaken," Pradeep replied, looking at the couple in the rearview mirror. "You are very much lucky to have a wife like her."

Danny and Valerie simultaneously turned to each other. Her face turned pink at the mere mention of them being married.

"I tell you what, I'll give you a fifty-dollar bonus if you wait for us while me and Miss Slumdog Millionaire get fitted for a party we're going to."

"That would be very great, sir," Pradeep said, parking the taxi in front of the bridal store.

THE STORE MANAGER WITH HIS protruding stomach greeted Danny and Valerie with a smile right away as they walked through the front door.

"You're here for pickup?" the manager asked.

"I hope they're ready," Valerie said.

The manager disappeared in the back. Valerie shifted her gaze at the rows upon rows of bridal gowns hanging on the racks. She envied the future brides who visited the store whenever they tried on one of the silky gowns. She thought of Pradeep's comment earlier. What he said echoed sweetly in her heart. She wondered if she was as pretty as those Bollywood actresses who danced their worries away to rhythmic Indian beats. She wondered if she'd ever walk down the aisle with a bouquet in hand, looking through the thin white veil on her way to the altar to meet Danny.

Through the window, Danny scanned the nearby parking lot for any sign of the two men who had been chasing them. He breathed a sigh of relief seeing nothing out of the ordinary.

When the manager returned, he was holding up a silky green bridesmaid gown with thin shoulder straps.

"Would you like to try it on?"

Valerie hung the gown over her arm and walked into the fitting room.

DANNY STOOD ON THE ELEVATED platform in front of the triple mirror and checked himself out in a slim-fitted black tuxedo. It fit perfectly. Adjusting the black cummerbund around his waist, he caught Valerie's reflection in the mirror as she glided back to him, her inner thighs peeking through the slit on the front of the dress. Danny turned around to greet her, noticing her dark green high heels—the end of the gown floating a few inches from the floor.

Valerie took a step up the platform and stood next to Danny. He bent his arm, and she took it. Studying their reflection in the mirror, her plunging neckline caught his attention. The V-shaped opening of her dress partly exposed her breasts. Danny could feel the heat of passion permeating in his loins as his eyes began to move down the depths of her cleavage.

VALERIE LOOKED AT HER REFLECTION with Danny standing next to her. She wished it could be the real deal, that she was standing at the altar in a pure white wedding gown, holding out her left hand while Danny placed the ring on her finger.

"I think we can fake our way into the party now," Valerie said, grinning.

TEN

THE WINDING ROAD OF VIA Capri was flanked with million-dollar mansions all across the mountainside of La Jolla. The copper sun was slowly dropping towards the horizon. The road shone with a golden sheen. Pradeep steered the taxi through the two-way street with confidence, rolling across shadows created by the tall trees.

"My GPS says we're here," Pradeep said, stopping the taxi in front of Dr. Adamson's mansion.

"We are indeed," Danny replied, eyeing the large stone-covered driveway filled with luxury cars.

"You are so very much kind sir," Pradeep said, handing Danny his business card. "Call me anytime and my services will be very much yours."

Danny pushed the door open and stepped out. As he marveled at the grand mansion, he wondered if Dr. Adamson could help.

After straightening his coat, he extended his hand and offered it to Valerie. She stuck her leg out the door and accepted it.

As if they were on a Saturday night date and not in a hurry to save a kidnapped friend from getting killed, Danny slowed his movements. He savored Valerie's elegant look, her cheeks highlighted with pink blush and her lips cherry red. Despite the pressing issues in front of them, they still found tender moments to appreciate the attraction permeating between them.

"You're lovely," Danny said, a smile spreading across his face.

"Thank you. You look handsome in your tailor-made tux," Valerie asserted.

Danny offered his arm, and Valerie took it. Slowly they made their way towards the party they were about to crash.

Danny stood at the door and stared at the large lion-head door knocker, wondering if he was doing the right thing. He had only met Dr. Adamson on a few occasions. Blake knew him better. Waiting for someone to answer the door, they could hear live jazz music vibrating through the side windows. Danny turned to Valerie. Her concerned expression mirrored his. Seeking help from someone who could help upload the data was good, but involving another person in their situation came with risks.

A man in his late fifties wearing a white coat and white gloves opened the door. Judging by the way he looked, Danny assumed it was the butler.

"Is Dr. Adamson available?" Danny asked.

A crinkle formed on the butler's forehead. He opened the door and ushered Danny and Valerie into the crowded living room. The butler waved his hand and a waiter approached them with a silver tray of champagne flutes. Danny took two glasses of bubbly and handed one to Valerie.

The butler excused himself, made an about-face, and left the room.

Danny turned to Valerie, taking a sip of his drink. Regret settled in the pit of his stomach, realizing the mistake he made of staying away from her for so long.

"You sure have rich friends," Valerie whispered, glancing at the naked sculpture in the middle of the living room.

"I don't know a single soul in this place."

"Looks like a bunch of snobs."

"I could never afford a palace like this. Especially not on a scientist's salary," Danny replied with a hint of disappointment in his voice.

"Someday. Who knows what the future has in store for you. When your invention is finally proven to work, it will make you millions," Valerie said with a hint of hope in her voice.

As Danny and Valerie waited for the butler to return, he marveled at the men and women in their expensive outfits wondering how they made their living and became so rich. Though he held his glass of champagne as if he was there to mingle with the other guests, he knew that they were there strictly for business.

Danny wanted to tell her that a million dollars wouldn't make any man happy without a woman to share his life with. He thought of how stupid he was for letting her go.

Helen was gone. Two years was enough time to spend wallowing in the past.

The time had come to turn his attention to Valerie.

VALERIE LOOKED UP AT THE high vaulted ceiling, in awe at the palatial size of the mansion. A slight breeze blowing from the open window lifted the ends of her hair.

She shifted her gaze to him with a deep longing. She wanted to tell him that she felt guilty for being indecisive and not telling him that they should carry on with what they felt for each other.

"When we get Elizabeth back, and this whole thing is over . . ." Danny said, lowering his glass.

Valerie was silent, anticipating the rest of his words.

Just as Danny was about to finish his thought, the butler came back.

"Dr. Adamson is ready to see you," the butler said, turning around and leading the way.

THE BUTLER OPENED THE DOOR to Dr. Adamson's library. The place was spacious with built-in, walnut-colored, floor-to-ceiling bookshelves filled with volumes and volumes on oceanography and marine biology. A massive executive-style desk was positioned near the back wall with a globe on one end and a lamp on the other. There was a painting of a Southern California scene. People were in a large room having a nice time as they listened to a man playing piano while palm trees swayed outside the window.

Danny was captivated by a bust of Julius Caesar, proudly resting on a pedestal. Next to the window was a telescope pointing up to the sky.

"The professor will be in soon." The butler walked out and closed the doors behind him.

The room became eerily quiet.

A few minutes later, the door on the side of the room opened. Dr. Adamson lumbered in with a cane. At age seventy, he looked distinguished with his dark brown hair, decorated by wisps of gray on the sides.

"Danny! I'm glad that you came for a visit," Dr. Adamson said, stopping a few feet away from him.

Though Dr. Adamson had been a United States resident for more than thirty years and had already assimilated into the American way of life, his English accent was still noticeable.

"Forgive us for just barging into your home on a very busy night without prior notice."

"Mi casa es su casa. You know that my doors are always open for you. And who might you be?" Dr. Adamson asked, turning to Valerie.

"My friend Valerie. She has been assisting me with a particular dilemma I'm in."

"I can tell that you're not here for caviar and champagne and to listen to the jazz quartet."

"That's what I like about you, Dr. Adamson. You cut to the chase and get right down to business."

"When you're running a multimillion-dollar research company, there's no time for subtleties except when I'm trying to extract donations from some of the snobs who are here tonight."

Danny cleared his throat and continued, "Just this morning, Blake and I received a call that his fiancée was kidnapped."

From the expression on his face, Dr. Adamson was shocked. "That's terrible news. Have you notified the authorities?"

"No . . . not yet. We were warned that if we did, Elizabeth would be killed."

"How can I help you? I know some people in high places. Do you want me to make some calls to help you get this resolved?"

"No, that's not why we're here. The kidnappers are demanding a thumb drive containing information about the fish migration data that was collected over the past six months."

"But isn't that only accessible in the company's secure server? If you came here wondering if I have access to it, I don't."

Dr. Adamson's revelation hit Danny like a brick. His hope of uploading the data without Blake's presence was torn away from him. Now, he was back to square one. To rendezvous with Blake was his only option.

"We have to upload the information before Elizabeth will be released."

"Data? People are willing to kill for that?"

"That's what's puzzling me. It only contains information about fish migration patterns, feeding schedules, water temperatures and field conditions."

"Do you have it with you?"

Danny fished the thumb drive from his front pocket, and with his open palm showed it to Dr. Adamson.

"How will you upload it?" Dr. Adamson asked, perplexed.

"Blake has a dedicated laptop with him."

"You can't get ahold of him or what?"

"I'm in contact with him, but every time we try to meet, we've got goons chasing us, two men with guns who seem like they'll do anything to disrupt us. Our phones have been hacked, and they're tracking our every move. They either want the thumb drive or our lives."

"You are welcome to stay here for the night if you need somewhere to hide out."

"Professor, since your company is one of the dozens of companies bidding for the exclusive rights to lure the fish to the protected grounds, I was wondering if you would let me use one of your computers?"

"But I thought you can only upload the data with dedicated company computers?"

"No, yours would be good enough, I just need to see the data. I need to figure out why these men are so adamant about obtaining the drive."

From a drawer, Dr. Adamson produced a laptop and placed it on the desk. Danny inserted the thumb drive. After pressing several commands, the screen lit up. An animated video began to play, simulating three motor vessels in the different parts of the Pacific Ocean. Behind them were red, blue and yellow dots representing fish. Danny's skin tingled when he saw a discrepancy in the telemetric data fed through the orbiting satellites. A week prior, he had seen the raw feed from out in the field and it didn't look like the image playing in front of him. The data on Ship #2 had been manipulated, and instead of leading the fish to the protected waters the ship was taking them elsewhere.

Ship #2 belonged to Dr. Adamson's company.

Danny slowly turned his head and saw Dr. Adamson's cold blue eyes looking at him with disdain.

"And now you know why those two men are trying to stop you from uploading the data on that thumb drive of yours," Dr. Adamson said as he placed his thumb under his chin. He reached for the office phone resting on the desk and pressed one of the buttons.

The side door clicked open.

The man with the ponytail who had been chasing Danny all morning entered the room with a menacing grin on his face.

"I believe you two have already met? This 'goon's' name is Yuri by the way, in case you need to know the name of the person who's going to kill you if you don't hand over the thumb drive," Dr. Adamson said.

"What's this all about?" Danny asked, his eyes widening. He stepped in front of Valerie, protecting her from Yuri. Instinctively, he pulled the thumb drive from out of the laptop.

"Give me the thumb drive before my associate dumps your bodies in the Tijuana River," Dr. Adamson commanded with his outstretched hand.

"You're the one who's been after us all day? Why did you kidnap Elizabeth? Why is this data so important to you?"

"I wasn't the one who ordered the kidnapping. Just give me the thumb drive and you two can leave unharmed."

"Why do you need it?"

"It's none of your concern," Dr. Adamson fired back with a sneer.

"If you take the thumb drive from me, all I have to do is call the police and report what you've done to us."

"First of all, who'd believe you? We're alone in this room, and no one can hear you. And also as an added bonus, if you run your mouth and snitch to the authorities, my associate here and his friends will come back and kill your lady friend. Can you live with that?"

Valerie's eyes widened in fear.

NOT WASTING ANY MORE TIME, Yuri steadfastly approached him, ready to pry the thumb drive from Danny's clenched fist.

Danny backed away from the maniac determined to do him harm, looking for a way out of the room.

IN THE MIDDLE OF THE chamber, Danny was in no man's land, far from anything he could use as a weapon. The situation was desperate.

Suddenly, his hip bumped into the desk. He groped for something with which to defend himself. He felt a round object with his right hand and grabbed it without even looking. Danny threw it straight at Yuri's face. As soon it left his hand, only then did he realize that it was just a baseball. Yuri ducked his head and charged at Danny. The ball missed Yuri and made a thudding sound as it knocked books off one of the wood shelves.

Danny sidestepped to avoid Yuri colliding into him, but his reaction wasn't quick enough. Yuri's head smashed into Danny's stomach and knocked the wind out of him. The impact was so hard that it pushed him several feet backward. While trying to regain his balance, Yuri quickly grabbed Danny by the shoulder and threw him down. The side of Danny's face slammed into the wooden floor, searing pain shooting through the side of his neck. It jarred him.

Wanting to do strike back, Danny rolled over Yuri and smashed the tip of his elbow deep into Yuri's ribcage. Unfortunately, it had little effect as the leather vest Yuri was wearing absorbed the impact. Yuri hardly cringed.

Yuri answered with a hard punch to Danny's temple and followed up by grabbing Danny's arm with one hard pull—Danny's chest banging on the floor. Finding the perfect opportunity, Yuri maneuvered on top of Danny and pinned him to the floor.

Not wanting to let the evil man destroy the man she cared about, Valerie rushed to Danny's aid. She spotted the telescope on the tripod. With no time to waste, she grabbed the entire setup. Just as she was about to smash it on Yuri's head, Dr. Adamson jammed the tip of his cane against her shoulder and followed up with a kick to her hip. She dropped the object just as she was thrown forward.

Danny tried to grab the telescope near him, but couldn't reach it. Yuri raised his fist over his head. Out the corner of his eye, Danny saw the deathblow coming towards him. Danny reacted quickly and turned to his side, shielding his face with his arms crossed in front of him. Yuri missed, his fist landing hard into the wooden floor.

"Fuck!" Yuri cried out in rage.

The thumb drive flew out of Danny's hand and tumbled across the floor. Yuri's eyes darted to where the thumb drive slid near the sofa. In that moment of distraction, Danny found the opportunity to push the monster off him and darted for the sofa to retrieve the drive. Recognizing what Danny was trying to do, Yuri dove for the thumb drive at the same time. Their shoulders slammed against each other. As Danny desperately reached for the thumb drive, Yuri grabbed his legs. Danny tried to wiggle out of his grip, but Yuri's hands were clamped around him like a vise. The thumb drive was only inches from his fingertips, but getting closer was impossible due to Yuri's unrelenting pull.

Desperate, Danny kicked hard. The bottom of his foot made contact on top of Yuri's head. Jarred by the impact, Yuri slackened his hold on Danny's leg.

Danny slithered forward. Finally, the thumb drive was back in his possession.

But Danny's victory was short-lived as he felt Yuri's massive weight slam into him. Yuri grabbed Danny's hand clutching the thumb drive and with his other hand tried to pry it open. Using the tip of his knuckles, Yuri drove them hard in between Danny's fingers. Danny screamed in agony. The thumb drive tumbled back onto the floor.

Danny could tell from Yuri's icy expression that Yuri wanted to eliminate him once and for all. Yuri hooked his right arm around Danny's neck, squeezing the air out of him. The veins across Danny's temples bulged. He tried to suck in air through his constricted windpipe, but with each passing second Yuri's grip became tighter. Danny desperately tried to loosen Yuri's chokehold, but to no avail.

Danny clenched his hand into a fist and swung it behind him hoping to land a solid punch on Yuri's jaw to knock the animal off him, but was unsuccessful. Yuri retaliated by snatching his arm, pulling it back and twisting it. Immediately, Danny felt searing pain shoot across his body. There was only so much he could take. He had to give in. He had to give up the thumb drive if he wanted to live.

Danny's eyes shot up to the ceiling above. His periphery began to darken. He could feel his body floating in space, and he began losing sensation in his fingertips. His skin was rapidly turning blue, his lips ashen.

As everything around Danny was turning into a sepia tone, he had the premonition that his death was imminent. Out of the blackening state, for some reason, images of the pristine beaches and coconut trees swaying in the wind in Philippines where he spent his childhood suddenly flooded his mind.

He thought of how short life could be and how it could end any day. For some strange reason, he felt OK. He wanted to save the world's fish populations so that generations to follow could enjoy the fruits of the sea, but it was not going to be on his watch. He tried dearly, but he had failed. He'd be dead in just a few seconds. Elizabeth, Blake and Valerie would follow.

His grip finally loosened. The thumb drive tumbled down to the floor.

WITH ONLY THE ADRENALINE POWERING her desire to survive the day, Valerie got up and rushed for the globe sitting on the desk. Sidestepping behind Yuri, she aimed for the back of his head. Just as she was about to drop it, Dr. Adamson yanked the back of her dress. The globe missed the top of Yuri's head, smashing into his left shoulder blade.

Yuri's grip slackened.

THE AIR THAT DANNY DESPERATELY needed came rushing back. His lungs expanded just as he was about to lose consciousness. His lips immediately returned to their pinkish hue. Danny hyperventilated, feeling a sudden surge of energy.

Danny slammed the back of his head into Yuri's nose. As a trail of bright red blood oozed down, Yuri's hands immediately went to his face. Danny turned sideways and delivered a sidekick to the man's lower abdomen.

Seizing the opportunity, Danny hammered the blade of his hand into Yuri's neck and followed up by swinging his fist right between his eyes. The blow was enough to knock him out.

WITH TWO GIANT STEPS, VALERIE flew across the room, bent down, and picked up the thumb drive. She was standing back up when Dr. Adamson came rushing towards her at full speed, slamming his shoulder in her upper back. She was thrown sideways. As she was trying to regain her stance, her elbow slammed into the edge of the desk and the thumb drive flew out of her hand.

Dr. Adamson seized the opportunity and rushed to take the drive into his possession. Danny pulled the rug under Dr. Adamson's feet. The feeble man lost his balance and fell down.

Quickly thinking, Valerie picked up the drive from the floor and stuffed it into her purse.

THE SIDE DOOR FLEW OPEN. Danny looked over to see the bald man barreling in at full force. Danny's heart sank. He'd used up all his energy to fight Ponytail and wasn't sure if he had what it took to defeat the big, bald man.

Igor slammed himself into the side of Danny's torso. The impact sent Danny colliding into the desk and falling to the ground. The bald man picked up the bust of Julius Caesar next to him. He was about to drop it on Danny's chest when Danny felt the telescope in his palm. Holding it like a baseball bat, he swung it hard and hit Baldy in the knees.

The bald man dropped the marble bust on his feet. A loud scream immediately followed.

Danny wasted no time and whipped Igor's arms and legs with the telescope.

FEELING DESPERATE WITH THE SUDDEN turn of events, Dr. Adamson swung his cane at Valerie's head, but it was no use. She caught his cane, grabbed him by his collar, and threw him to the floor, where he landed hard on his hip. He was no match for Valerie's agility and strength.

"Come on, let's get out of here!" Danny yelled, swiping the laptop from the desk.

THE LABYRINTH OF THE MANSION'S hallways was dizzying as Danny and Valerie searched for a way out. Although running back towards the party was the logical option, Dr. Adamson's security team might have already been alerted and ready to nab them. They would not be able to fight such a large force. Slipping out the back without raising any suspicion would be for the best.

"How do we get out of here?" Valerie asked through her panicked breaths.

"I don't know," Danny sputtered. "I've only been here once. You're the architect, what do you think?"

Valerie thought of the thousands of home designs she had remodeled throughout her career. She knew that the mansion's style of architecture usually had several back doors. Through the window, Valerie could see the luxury cars parked outside. She remembered seeing one of the guests handing his car key to one of the valets earlier.

"We need to get to the cars parked on the side," Valerie suggested.

"You mean steal one?"

"I wouldn't put it that way. We're just borrowing it from the owner without his permission."

Danny mulled over Valerie's harebrained idea. As absurd as it might sound, it was probably their only way out of getting killed by the killers searching for them.

At the end of the hallway was a large door. Thinking it would lead both of them outside, Valerie pulled it open. His heart sank when he found only a dimly lit art studio.

"Wrong room," Danny pointed out.

"We need to check all the doors to see where they lead us," Valerie replied, already backing up.

But they stopped in their tracks when they heard the sound of loud footsteps echoing in the hallway.

"They're here. Get inside," Danny whispered, nudging Valerie forward and closing the door behind him.

The floor was covered in canvas drop cloths. Unfinished art pieces sat on wooden easels. Buckets filled with paintbrushes sat side by side on paint-splattered tables.

Anticipating that that the two men would be walking in at any moment, he searched the darkened room for a place to hide. They were rounding the drafting table to get behind some large art pieces when the doorknob began to click open.

"Danny," Valerie whispered in panic.

"Quick . . . duck and hide behind here." Danny pointed to the large desk.

Valerie crouched down on her hands and knees. Danny plucked a palette knife from a bucket of art tools to use as a weapon and dropped to the floor.

Through the slit between the canvas and the table, Danny saw Yuri limp into the room, the bald man following closely. The two of them spread across the room inspecting each nook.

Yuri shouted something to the bald man. Though Danny couldn't understand what he was saying, it looked like Igor was being ordered to find the light switch as he started groping across the wall.

Danny shot a glance at Valerie who was taking slow breaths and trying not to make any noise. He pressed his back against the wall, ready to defend himself and Valerie in case they were discovered.

Yuri accidentally kicked one of the tall easels in his path. The large canvas fell on the floor. The loud crash reverberated throughout the room. Valerie's eyes widened in alarm. Danny could tell from the expression in her face that her heart leapt to her throat. Danny reached for her hand to calm her.

Danny peeked around the canvas to see what the two were doing. Yuri immediately picked the artwork off the floor, sat it upright, and propped it against the table. Igor walked a few feet past them. Danny traced Yuri's hand all the way to his forearm and saw a menacing skull tattoo. Yuri was so close that Danny could smell the sour odor of his unwashed body mixed with the ashy stink of tobacco. His blood pressure spiked, knowing it could be the end of his quest to save Elizabeth if they were discovered.

The phone clipped to Igor's waist started to vibrate. He answered it, nodding several times. Ending the call, Igor yelled something from across the room. The two men walked out.

The room suddenly became quiet.

"I think they're gone," Valerie whispered.

Danny slowly rose from behind the easels for a clearer view. With only half of his face sticking out from the edge of the stretched canvas, he surveyed the room for any sign of the two men. Confident that they were alone, he extended his hand to Valerie and pulled her up.

"They might still be in the hallway. Turn your phone on," Danny said.

"But those men will track us," Valerie protested.

"They already know we're here. Besides, I don't think the cell sites can pinpoint our exact location. I'll turn it off as soon as I find out where they are."

Danny picked up a five-foot dowel and a roll of a blue painter's tape lying on the table. He placed the smartphone at the end of the stick and wrapped the tape around it. Twisting the phone sideways, fitting it under the door, he used it like a periscope. Pointing it down the hallway, he began recording, searching for any trace of the two men.

"Do you see anything?" Valerie asked.

"Looks like it's clear," Danny said, watching the playback.

Valerie slowly opened the door, avoiding any creaking sounds that might give them away. Danny and Valerie tiptoed into the hallway hoping to escape. With luck on their side, the first door that Valerie opened led them directly out the side of the mansion. From across the grassy patch, Danny could see the cars parked side by side. Danny started to run, but Valerie grabbed his hand.

"Slow down, we'll draw attention."

He heeded her warning.

In front of them were shiny new luxury sedans and sports cars. Danny peeked inside a dark blue SUV, wanting to find out if the key was still in the ignition. The valets were all by the entrance; he was out of their line of sight. If they could get into the vehicle as soon as possible, the chances of being detected would be slim behind the tinted windows.

He was about to pull the driver-side door open when Valerie started to scream.

"Danny!"

Danny saw Yuri charging in their direction, Igor a few paces behind.

Getting in the SUV, starting it, and backing away would take at least a few minutes. Precious time was being wasted. They could be looking straight into the muzzle of a pistol at any second. Danny assessed their surroundings for a place to escape. The back of the mansion was facing a cliff, heading that way would be a deathtrap. The only logical thing to do in order to get away from the thugs was to get back inside the mansion. With the situation getting desperate, Danny thought of dialing 9-1-1 and hiding among the hundreds of guests while they waited for the police to arrive. It seemed like the only way for them to escape the mansion. The authorities would question them, but at least they would be alive.

It was the last thing he wanted to do because he'd be forced to tell them everything. Elizabeth's life could be jeopardized if the authorities got too involved.

With the situation deteriorating every second, he felt that they had no other choice but to run.

"To the mansion, now!" Danny shouted.

VALERIE PULLED OPEN THE FIRST door she found, surprised to see that it led to the main kitchen. A dozen or so cooks stood busy, preparing the meals that were getting sent out to the guests.

Danny and Valerie had just run past the prep table when the door blew open. The two men barged in, immediately spotting them. Danny pulled down a stack of dishes, porcelain shattering across the smooth tile floor. The sound overpowered the already noisy kitchen staff barking orders to one another.

Danny and Valerie fled, searching for any open door.

THE MANSION WAS SIMPLY TOO big. Neither Danny nor Valerie had any idea where to go. Going out the front door was impossible as the security guards had likely already been alerted, so they headed to the garage.

As she opened the door to her left, her face wrinkled in disappointed to find the laundry room.

Danny opened the door to his right, glad to find the garage they were looking for. A red convertible, a pickup truck, and a motorcycle were all parked inside.

Danny looked in the convertible for a key, but found nothing. Valerie stuck her head through the pickup truck's passenger side door checking if the key was inside, but had no luck. Danny pulled the driver-side door open, lifted the floor mat, and pulled down the visor hoping that a spare key would fall out, but there was none.

"Fuck!" Danny cursed under his breath. "No key."

"Danny," Valerie said, pointing to the motorcycle. "The key is in the ignition."

The last time Danny drove a two-wheeled vehicle was when he was on holiday in Italy, and that was a scooter—a much less powerful machine than this 750cc crotch rocket that could go from zero to sixty in less than six seconds.

"Can you drive this?" Valerie asked, sounding scared.

Though Danny preferred having four wheels, it wasn't an option at the moment. If he wanted to get away, he had to do it. Danny turned to her and with reassurance in his voice replied, "Put on a helmet. We need to go."

Valerie hit the garage door switch. Danny hopped on the bike and turned the ignition. Valerie jumped on behind him, pulled her skirt up, and sat on the excess hem so that it wouldn't get caught in the chain.

Danny bent forward as if ready to attack. He raised the kickstand with the back of his heel and balanced the motorcycle into the upright position. Squeezing the clutch, he shifted to first gear. With all his weight, he kick-started the motor. The bike roared to life. He released the clutch with his left hand and revved the engine.

"Hang on!" Danny shouted.

Valerie planted her feet on the footrest, wrapped her arms tight around Danny's waist, and pressed her cheek against his back, hanging on for dear life.

The motorcycle lurched forward as the back of the bike wobbled. The black tires spun wildly, leaving behind smoke and the smell of burnt rubber. They flew down the driveway towards their freedom on the open road.

ELEVEN

AS THEY HEADED UPHILL, DANNY saw the reflection of a red sports car driving erratically in his side view mirror. Chills shot all the way to his fingertips knowing that the two men were in pursuit. He checked the options on how to evade his pursuers. He saw a plastic figure of a man in a hat holding a red triangular flag warning drivers to slow down because kids were at play. Wanting to avoid an accident, he turned right to a wide street leading up the mountain.

He switched gears and twisted the throttle. His speed increased, but the car was getting even closer. Hearing gunshots, he turned the handlebar left and right, weaving to try to avoid the bullets flying at them. The motorcycle darted in and out of the lane, crossing the double yellow lines in the middle of the asphalt road. He revved the engine, squeezed the clutch, and switched to a higher gear for more speed. The three-stroke motor let out an angry scream. The tires bit the asphalt for traction and his speed increased. He lowered his head and pointed the top of his helmet into the wind for better aerodynamics. Added speed was essential for their escape. He felt Valerie's arms tighten around his waist. Her cheek pressed hard into his shoulder blades as she fought against being thrown off her seat. The faster he drove through the two-lane streets, the harder it was for him to see what was coming in front of him. The entire motorcycle started shaking, and the handlebars became harder to control. And yet the only thing he could do was to go even faster.

As more and more asphalt disappeared behind him, Danny became desperate not knowing where to turn to escape. His surroundings were quickly becoming more and more unfamiliar as mansion-sized houses built along the side of the mountain appeared. With the setting sun shining on his face, he realized that heading to the beach area would be the best way to hide, its streets flooded with tourists.

From the side view mirror he saw the sloping hood of the red sports car. He didn't know where to turn. It seemed impossible to lose the two men chasing them on the two-lane road. As he was coming around the bend, he was distressed to see a blue sedan puttering up the mountain pass directly in front of him. Danny tilted his head up and scanned the road for oncoming cars.

The last thing he wanted was to lock the brakes and spin out of control, so he swung the bike into the oncoming lane.

Just as he was about to pass the car in front of him, a water-delivery truck appeared in the horizon, barreling straight for Danny.

"Watch out!" Valerie shouted.

He decided that passing the car was his only option. The right shoulder had enough space but Danny knew it was far more dangerous to pass on that side. It was hard to estimate the truck's distance. He looked down at his speedometer. The needle was pushing close to seventy miles per hour. He wasn't sure if adding more gas would speed up the motorcycle since they were on an uphill turn.

Though the double yellow line represented no passing, he ignored the basic traffic rule and crossed it in order of outrun the pursuing men. He followed the yellow strips like a ribbon flowing in the wind. His jacket flapped on his side. The wind pushed Valerie's skirt back revealing the smooth skin of her legs. The top of Valerie's green dress blew open, her cleavage exposed.

Following the curve of the ascending road, Danny leaned into the turn. Valerie shifted her weight with Danny's lead. The motorcycle was leaning so close to the ground that their knees were almost touching the asphalt. It was a risky maneuver that could cause them to slip off the road and crash, but he had no choice.

Danny could sense from Valerie's tight embrace that she shut her eyes as she hung on for dear life. He wished he could find a way to get them out of the jam they were in, but there seemed to be no end in sight.

Having no more space on the left and with the car just inches away on his right, he did the unthinkable. He twisted the throttle and shifted to a higher gear instead of decreasing their speed and hiding behind the car. Seeing that the road was clear, he swung the bike into oncoming traffic. The engine took in more air, and the pistons worked double time. Valerie slid a few inches back but kept her hold around Danny. The crotch rocket lived up to its name, launching itself forward like a rocket blasting into outer space.

The wind blew hard in his face. The tips of Valerie's hair sticking out of her helmet fluttered uncontrollably. They were back on the open road as the needle in his speedometer pushed past 100 miles per hour.

AS HE WAS NEARING THE end of the road, Danny saw that it came to a three-way junction. The only way to escape the sports car was to turn right down Soledad Mountain Road and toward Pacific Beach. There would be lots of streets where he could lose Yuri and Igor.

Danny was about to turn right when a black SUV blocked his path. Avoiding a violent collision, he jerked the handlebar to the left and applied the brakes, narrowly missing the car's back bumper. The motorcycle shook violently out of control. He put his foot down to prevent the bike from tipping over.

He was able to regain balance right away.

Finding a small sliver of space between the large van and the mountain, Danny downshifted and throttled up. The front wheel lifted a few inches off the ground. The tires screeched on the asphalt leaving white smoke behind.

His quick thinking saved them from crashing into the van, but his victory was snuffed out of him as soon as he saw the tip of a white cross. He was heading straight up Mount Soledad. And with their pursuers close behind, Danny realized that they were trapped.

It was a dead end.

With no other choice, he continued up until reaching the top of the horseshoe-shaped road. He noticed gray plaques bearing the names of fallen soldiers from past wars. If he didn't think of a way out, real fast, he'd be in the same situation as those heroes.

He faced the motorcycle downhill and idled the engine as he waited for the two men. He formulated a plan. As soon as the red sports car came up to them, he would launch into a fast descent down the road to evade his potential captors. If the car approached them on the left side, he'd go down on the right. He looked out into the distance. Cars speeding by hummed on the freeway below. It was where he needed to make his escape. As he waited for the car to arrive, he wished that his motorcycle had been equipped with a pair of wings so that he could fly through the low-hanging clouds and over the gray-blue sea.

Danny was surprised about what transpired next.

The sports car stopped at the entrance right in the middle where the road split. The doors started to open, and out of one came a rifle barrel.

"My god!" Valerie cried.

He revved the motor and shifted gears.

"Hang on tight!" Danny shouted, grasping for Valerie's hand and kissing it.

With terror in her voice, Valerie cautioned, "I don't think it's a good idea!"

"We have no choice!"

He released the clutch lever and twisted the throttle. The engine screamed, and the motorcycle took off. Valerie pressed her chest tight against Danny's back, squeezing the laptop in between to secure it from flying off.

In less than four seconds, they were flying down the narrow road at fifty miles per hour.

YURI AND IGOR WERE JUST getting out of the car when the high-pitched sound of the motorcycle engine caught their attention. Their eyes widened in surprise with Danny's audacity. Straight ahead, Danny was headed at them at high speed. Igor cocked the gun and aimed at Danny's chest to kill him on the spot. He pulled the trigger. Bullets exploded out of the muzzle.

Danny steered the bike from side to side, avoiding a direct hit. Igor followed his target, but couldn't land a clean shot on either Danny or the motorcycle's engine. He missed hitting any part of the two-wheeled machine. It was simply going way too fast, even though the motorcycle was only a few feet in front of him. The bullets flew out into the sapphire San Diego sky.

DANNY AIMED THE MOTORCYCLE DIRECTLY at the car. Just as they were about to crash into the front hood, he pulled on the handlebars and shifted his weight back. The front wheel lifted up and smashed hard onto the shiny hood.

With the slope of the sports car's front hood, it acted like a ramp. As the motorcycle rolled over the car it crushed the windshield, cracking it into a thousand pieces. The metal roof crunched under the weight of the motorcycle, leaving a groove.

QUICKLY REACTING TO THE SITUATION, Yuri shot at the bike's motor attempting to disable and sending it to a fiery crash.

Yuri was too late.

The motorcycle was already zooming away.

ANTICIPATING THAT BULLETS WERE SOON coming at them, Danny immediately steered the front wheel to his left and back to the road. When both wheels landed back on the ground, through the reflection on the side view mirror, Danny saw the white cross fading behind them.

ALTHOUGH LA JOLLA WAS ONE of the most beautiful spots in San Diego County, Danny found the streets confusing. There would be plenty of places to hide, but at the same time Danny was not sure where to go. After driving for ten minutes, Danny eased up on the throttle and slowed the motorcycle as soon as he determined that he had lost the two men. He pushed himself up a bit and straightened his back to ease his tense muscles.

With the wind blasting in his face easing up, he flipped his visor up and unbuttoned his tuxedo blazer to dry the perspiration that had drenched his body. The wind was soft in his face. He felt his pulse calm down, confident that the men chasing him were far away. But it wasn't time to celebrate yet. The killers could appear anytime like they had before, so he pressed on wanting to get as far away as he could.

Danny found himself driving on Nautilus Street. With the sun warming his face, he was confident that he was heading westbound and would be in the heart of La Jolla soon. And with the web of avenues intersecting at different points and streets that ended in cul-de-sacs, there were plenty of places to hide until he and Valerie could figure out what to do next.

He thought of going all the way to Windansea Beach, sending a cryptic message to Blake, and meeting him at the surfer's hut so they could upload the data. On early mornings, Danny would meet with Blake to go surfing there. If he sent the message now, he was sure that Blake would understand what he meant and meet him there right away. He contemplated if his plan would work. The solution seemed to be so easy. Besides, if the two goons showed up, they could be trapped.

Instead, he turned northbound.

La Jolla Boulevard came to a dead end on Coast Boulevard. Danny followed the two-lane road, passing the cars parked along the curb. He shot a glance to his left. Tourists were taking selfies on the cliff with the beach behind them. Lovers with their arms wrapped around each other were tucked in between the webbings of rocks reaching into the beach, waves splashing onto the fine sand.

He drove past the La Jolla Children's Pool, overtaken by seals sunbathing in the sand.

THE ROAD EVENTUALLY CONNECTED WITH Prospect Street. The famous street lined with restaurants, bars and galleries was filling up with the late afternoon crowd. He wished he and Valerie were sitting in a farm-to-table restaurant, relaxing and enjoying a cold glass of Riesling paired with a toasted baguette and a garlic butter spread.

Finally, he made it to the onramp of the Interstate 5 freeway. There was a line of cars waiting on the metered ramp. He tapped his brakes and slowed down.

"Please get my phone. I need to call Blake," Danny requested, turning his head to Valerie.

VALERIE SLID HER HAND DOWN Danny's front pocket searching for his phone. The last time her hands were gliding along his thighs was that night when they were alone and naked in a hotel room. She began to reminisce about that sweet afternoon filled only with love and desire.

From their rented cottage at Mission Beach, the ninety-year-old wooden roller coaster was only a stone's throw away. Valerie could hear the riders screaming in excitement.

Men in board shorts played volleyball on the beach as women in bikinis rollerbladed along the boardwalk with their headphones on. Families sat around fire pits enjoying the warmth of their bonfires.

Their lips were already locked when they reached the front of their rental. As soon as Danny slammed the door shut, Valerie was already unbuckling Danny's belt while he undid her bra. He planted a kiss on her navel, sliding his tongue along the supple line that went all the way to her breasts.

Danny slowly slithered his hands over her extended arms until his hands met hers. Their fingers curled together. Fully naked now, Danny led her to the bed. She spread her legs. Danny wasted no time and guided his being inside her. As he entered her, Valerie felt the electrical circuits inside her brain going haywire, overloading her senses. With each passionate thrust, Valerie's insides exploded with delight. There was nothing she could do but to curl her fingers in the satin sheets.

Danny was so gentle with her, yet in so much control. She could feel his manhood and her body reacted with a spasm of elation.

There was nothing for her to do but experience that moment with reckless abandon. She felt the heat rising from the bottom of her belly. It was almost too much to bear—feeling Danny's warm skin, the flat plane of his chest pressing against her breasts.

Danny buried his face on the side of her neck, inhaling her scent.

Then, with the last final thrust he drove deep inside her. She cried out in pleasure and satisfaction as Danny moaned. Valerie felt her nerve fibers quake. She grasped Danny's buttocks and pressed him deep inside her.

"I got it," Valerie shouted through her helmet.

"Press Blake's speed dial."

Through his earpiece, Danny heard Blake's voice crackle on the other line.

"Leave now and hide!" Danny yelled. "Dr. Adamson hired those goons who are trying to nab us."

"But isn't his company one of the ones bidding for the contract?" Blake asked, sounding perplexed.

"No time to explain. He is manipulating the fish results. I was just at his mansion fighting the two guys chasing us. They tried to kill Valerie and me. Go deep until I sort this out. Wait for my text tomorrow morning."

The line went dead.

Valerie shut off the phone and slipped it back in his front pocket.

When the light finally turned green, Danny switched gears and joined the sea of vehicles going northbound on Interstate 5, not knowing where to go next.

"**WHAT DO YOU HAVE?**" **YURI** asked, focusing on the road in front of him through the windshield of the car Yuri had carjacked earlier from a tourist at Mount Soledad.

"I just got a ping from the cell towers. Triangulating now," Igor replied, concentrating on the laptop screen.

"I need to know now so I can steer in their direction."

"The motherfucker turned his phone off. The signal died."

"Where's their last known position?"

"They're heading northbound on the Interstate 5," Igor said, folding the laptop screen.

Yuri placed both of his hands on top of the steering wheel, focused on the road in front of him with intensity. A slight sneer zipped across his face, satisfied how stupid Danny was for turning his phone on despite being monitored. He was aware that Danny's need to communicate with Blake was vital, and that it would be Danny's weakness. It was hard to spot how far away the motorcycle was, but Yuri understood that Danny and Valerie weren't too far ahead. He needed to get closer to Danny so he could end the chase and take the thumb drive—and perhaps, as an added bonus, kill him on the spot. Having wasted so many opportunities, this time he was determined not to make any more mistakes. He should have captured him a long time ago.

Yuri ejected the empty clip from his pistol. Reaching for a full magazine from his belt, he slapped it in the gun and cocked it. He was intent on emptying the magazine onto the motorcycle until it was down to the ground and Danny's arms and legs were splayed on the freeway.

Like a birthday gift that had fallen into his lap, he spotted Valerie's green dress flapping behind the black motorcycle as it sped between the lanes. He gunned the engine, and the eight-cylinder car picked up speed. Black smoke rushed out the tail pipe as the tires spun faster, pushing the car past ninety miles per hour. With a pickup truck driving slowly in front of him, Yuri quickly changed lanes and cut in front of a station wagon. The driver behind him honked his horn.

DANNY HEARD THE LONG DRONING sound of the horn. He shifted his eyes to the side view mirror. From out of nowhere, an orange muscle car suddenly appeared from behind the other cars like an apparition, weaving in and out of the lanes. At first, he thought it was just a figment of his imagination. Then all hell broke loose when he saw a pistol sticking out of the window. Danny hit the gas.

"Hold on tight. They're right behind us!"

Danny concentrated on the freeway in front of him dotted with buttons and long dashes of white lines. If he didn't think of a way of out running the men chasing him, it would be his ruination.

Along the freeway was the green exit sign. He was approaching an off-ramp. He thought of exiting so he could throw them off and lose them permanently. It was too risky. There was only one way, and they could be trapped.

Danny aimed for the apex of the fork where the lane they were on split in two. One continued to the freeway, the other one to the off-ramp. He relaxed his grip on the throttle. The motorcycle slowed down.

"What are you doing?" Valerie shouted through the wind.

"I'm letting them catch up to us," Danny replied without taking sight on his objective.

"You're going to do what?!" Valerie questioned in disbelief. "We'll be in shooting range!"

YURI WAS SURPRISED AGAIN BY Danny's audacity, always pushing the envelope to get away from him. He stepped on the clutch, shifted to fourth gear, and stepped on the gas. The car lurched forward with determination.

The six-stroke engine screamed, sucking in more air and burning more gas as it pushed the pistons to work even harder.

"What the fuck is he doing?" Igor shouted as he aimed his pistol at the motorcycle's rear tire.

From Yuri's vantage point, Danny was going to slam straight into the end of the guardrail where the crash cushions were positioned, just before the freeway split off to the exit. Yuri couldn't tell if Danny was intending to head to the off-ramp or join the flow of cars on the freeway. He did what was necessary and followed the speeding motorcycle wanting to end his quest.

Just as Danny was about to reach the guard rail, he slowed down.

DANNY SAW THE ORANGE MUSCLE car getting bigger in the mirror. Carrying out the plan he formulated in his head, he downshifted and hit the brakes. The motorcycle's back wheel slightly lifted as its speed rapidly decreased a few feet just before the exit. The bike started wavering from side to side. Trying to regain control, he squeezed the clutch and downshifted.

Danny aimed the handlebar straight to the exit ramp.

A GRIN FLASHED IN YURI'S face. Instead of slowing down, he reacted by stepping harder on the gas pedal, intending to plow straight into Danny's motorcycle.

Yuri, anticipating Danny's evasive action, turned the steering wheel to the right.

Just as the front of the car was about to slam into the motorcycle's back tire, Danny suddenly steered back onto the freeway, the front tire narrowly missing the end of the guardrail. Yuri reacted quickly and jerked the steering wheel to the left. But he miscalculated, unable to see that he was headed straight for the yellow-marked tip of the guardrail where the impact attenuators were strategically positioned. Trying to maintain control, Yuri slammed on his brakes, but the force of the car's momentum sent it skidding for the off-ramp. The tires lost their grip on the smooth surface of the concrete freeway. Yuri lost control of the vehicle. As the car's front bumper crashed into the impact attenuator, its speed topping 100 miles per hour, it bent the guardrail into unrecognizable pieces of metal.

UNFORTUNATELY, BECAUSE DANNY WANTED YURI and Igor to get as close to him as possible to make his move more unpredictable, he now had only had a few inches between himself and their car. As the guardrail was coming off its brackets, it snagged the chain of Valerie's clutch bag. As he sped off, the chain snapped from the force of the motorcycle. Her bag tumbled onto the side of the freeway. Danny aimed the motorcycle back onto the highway, following the solid white line. From his side view mirror, he saw the sports car in mangled pieces.

THE CAR STOPPED RIGHT OVER the clutch bag. Gasoline, brake fluid and radiator fluid started leaking. Realizing the gravity of their situation, Igor unbuckled himself right away, then Yuri shortly thereafter. They needed to get out of there immediately. As they ran from the wreckage, a spark from the engine ignited the gasoline. Fire shot up in the air, burning the custom-made muscle car and the thumb drive that was the key to Elizabeth's freedom.

Stranded on the freeway, Yuri and Igor could only watch Danny and Valerie as they sped away.

TWELVE

APPROXIMATELY TWENTY MILES NORTH OF down-town San Diego and a few miles south of the famous Del Mar racetrack lay Torrey Pines State Beach. Danny lowered the kickstand and parked the motorcycle near the boulders that served as barriers to the water.

Taking his helmet off, he threw it to the ground. "I can't believe this shit! We've lost the thumb drive. I shouldn't have made that stupid maneuver."

Valerie stepped closer to Danny, comforting him. "It's not your fault. You did what you had to do to get us out of danger."

"Yeah . . . we're alive, but Elizabeth will be dead tomorrow night."

"There has to be another copy somewhere."

Danny looked at the different layers of the sandstone cliffs turning ochre with the late afternoon sun. The beach was mostly empty, lacking the usual hubbub of beachgoers getting their tans. Below him, a lifeguard rescue vehicle was slowly rolling along, leaving wheel marks on the sand. Kids were crouched down touching the amber-colored kelp that had washed ashore. He turned his head to the shore, as if the answer to their dilemma would surface from the crashing waves.

"Let's sit over there while we figure out what to do next," Valerie said, pointing to the aqua-green lifeguard station directly in front of them.

Danny climbed down, stepping carefully on the large boulders. He turned around and offered his hand to Valerie. She kindly accepted his gesture of courteousness. Her hand felt soft. He remembered the first time when they were walking along the pier in Pacific Beach—holding hands as they passed by the locals fishing—their poles propped on the rail as they waited for a catch. The surfers in their wetsuits sat on their boards waiting for the next big wave. Everything around them was calm. There wasn't a care in the world.

Danny and Valerie climbed up the lifeguard tower. They sat on the platform and looked out at the sun as it was about to kiss the horizon. The low clouds in the vast sky seemed as if they didn't want to float away.

WITH THE OCEAN BREEZE GETTING cooler, Danny placed his arm around her shoulder and pulled her tight against the side of his body. Valerie was surprised with Danny's move, but she didn't mind. She had been longing for his embrace. It was nice to feel his skin pressing against her own once again. She felt good next to Danny—the man she'd always wanted to be with.

They were silent. She shifted her sights to the Torrey Pines State Reserve. She could see the outline of the rare Torrey pines standing tall on top of the ridge. A puff of wind blew from the ocean, playing with Valerie's hair. She pushed her hair with her fingers from the side of her face and breathed in the cool damp air, hoping it would calm her raging nerves.

"We need to figure out where to stay for the night. Our house is being watched," Danny said through the rumble of waves crashing on the shore.

Hotels were out of the question. Such places required identification. Yuri and Igor would be at their doorstep faster than the room service.

"You took me once to a cottage in Oceanside your aunt owned."

"You're right. I can stay there anytime as long as it's vacant," Danny replied.

With the only ambient light slipping away behind the wall of ocean, Valerie knew there wasn't much they could do this late in the day. They needed somewhere safe to stay alive through one more night. She thought of Elizabeth spending another terrifying night in her glass tank filling with water and Blake alone and worried sick for his fiancée, clueless as to whether or not she or Danny were still alive. As much as Valerie wanted their terrible situation to be over, there wasn't much she could do.

She watched Danny as he pushed the motorcycle upright and slipped his helmet on. Valerie sat behind him and wrapped her arms around his waist. Checking for oncoming traffic, Danny made a quick U-turn and continued north.

THEY NEEDED CASH AND NEW clothes. Although it was risky to make a withdrawal, Danny decided to stop by an ATM in Encinitas—a seaside city further north of San Diego. Like locals joyriding, they drove along the South Coast Highway, passing by pizzerias and surf shops.

Danny parked the motorcycle behind a bank and walked up to the ATM. Though he wanted to take out more cash, he could only withdraw the maximum amount the bank would allow. Stuffing three hundred dollars in his pocket, he hoped that it would be enough to cover their costs for the night.

The outlet mall in Carlsbad was crowded with Friday night shoppers when Danny and Valerie arrived. His jacket was nearly falling apart and her dress was torn at the bottom from running all afternoon and from the wind blasting her. They needed to go shopping to get out of their damp clothes.

After picking out a comfortable pair of jeans, two T-shirts, and a pair of rubber-soled shoes, Danny went straight to the fitting room. He locked the door behind him. The silence inside gave him a few minutes to contemplate what to do next. At that moment, he felt lost. He curled his fingers and pounded the bench he sat on in frustration that their situation was even worse than when they had started. In the comfort of his private room, he rolled up his ripped tuxedo jacket along with his tattered pants and dumped them in the waste bin. He could now move freely in his new clothes.

About ten minutes later, Valerie came out of the fitting room, wearing tight-fitting jeans that highlighted the curves of her hips, matched with a white button-down blouse, a thin black jacket, and ankle-high boots. Danny was stunned by her new look.

"I almost didn't recognize you," Danny said, walking to the cashier.

Thirteen

Danny picked up the jar hidden in the garden behind the cottage. The thick fragrance of jasmine and roses lingered in the vicinity. He unscrewed the lid and a key tumbled down into his palm. With a side glance, he winked at Valerie. She returned it with a half-smile.

"No one knows about this place. We can chill here until we figure out our next move," Danny said, unlocking the back door.

The cottage was approximately 500 square feet with a single bedroom, a small living room and a small kitchen. Valerie opened the cabinets, glad to find them well stocked with canned goods. She turned to the refrigerator, pulled out the drawers and found some cheese and prosciutto.

Danny walked over to the large glass window in the living room facing the ocean. Pushing the blinds down, he peeked outside. He worried that the two hired killers were in the periphery and might have already tracked them down. The tourists on Oceanside Pier were leaning on the railing, watching the surfers. Mothers sauntered along the concrete walkway, pushing strollers. For a second, he wished Valerie was one of them with a child of their own. Imagining their daily routine, Danny could easily see their potential life together. He and Valerie would come home from work and have dinner together, sitting at the table while their child picked up bits of cereal off the lap tray. He would tell himself how lucky he'd been for having a woman like her.

Danny was happy to find frozen *lumpias*—Filipino-style egg rolls—sitting in the freezer, ones that his aunt made herself whenever she had time. He knelt on the floor and pulled out the bottom shelf, glad to see tomatoes, a head of lettuce and a bunch of spinach.

"I found a bag of tortilla chips and some canned beans," Valerie said. "I'll heat up the beans."

It was as if they never had separated and had just picked up where they left off. They felt comfortable being alone together in such an enclosed space. If there were issues just before Danny and Valerie parted ways, they did well to ignore the awkwardness of the situation. As he chopped the tomatoes, for a brief moment he pretended that he was playing the part of a happy husband who had just come home to his loving wife.

While Danny waited for the pot filled with cooking oil to heat up, he thought of telling Valerie how much he'd missed her and how stupid he was for walking away. He wanted to ask her if she thought of him often. He came closer to her. The light coming through the window lit up the side of her face. Danny gazed at her. The thought of touching her smooth cheeks and kissing her on the lips crossed his mind, but he debated if the timing was right.

Valerie turned to him as she sprinkled cheese on the hot beans.

"Do you want to use the sink?" Valerie asked, diffusing the growing tension between them.

"I just need a bowl," Danny said.

Valerie reached for it and passed it to Danny. Their fingertips brushed together. Brief as it was, the contact sent a spark arching across his fingertips. Danny was surprised to see her already staring into his dark brown eyes. Valerie immediately looked away, timid.

He placed the big bowl of salad and the plate of deep-fried lumpia on the table next to the beans and chips. For a second he admired the simple but satisfying foods he loved. A perfect marriage of Filipino and Mexican dishes.

The setting sun painted the small dining room with an orange hue. Through the narrow slit in the blinds, Danny saw a barefoot couple walking along the edge of the waves on the beach. Just a few months ago they were like those two people, with Valerie pressed against him and her thumb hooked on his back pocket.

He watched Valerie pour sweet and sour sauce into a small dish. Besides the fact that she was beautiful, it was those little things she did for him that made him attracted to her even more. She could have dated any man she wanted, especially after Danny told her that he needed to some time off.

He was glad she didn't.

"I trusted Dr. Adamson. I can't believe that he'd been manipulating the data reports coming from the field," Danny commented, pouring chilled Moscato into the two wine glasses on the table.

"Greed makes people forget their morals."

"Yeah, but he heads several committees on ocean safety. Why would his ship divert the fish away from the protected waters to who knows where?"

"Is he making a lot of money from these operations?"

"Not much while the experiments are going on."

"And if he gets the contract?" Valerie asked, placing loose lettuce and sliced tomatoes on Danny's plate.

"With several countries already pledging millions toward saving the fish population and more funds to come, he could make millions."

Valerie bit into a piece of lumpia.

"How many companies are bidding for the contract?"

"There's five. Three foreign companies—one French, one Norwegian and one Japanese. Two are American."

"What's the other American company?

"It's a local company owned by Dr. Tran. He also has a background in marine biology."

"Is it safe to say that Dr. Tran and Dr. Adamson are fierce competitors?"

"Not only that, they hate each other with every fiber in their bodies. They have been accusing each other of stealing patents for years. Why . . . what's on your mind?"

"You've heard of the saying, 'The enemy of my enemy is my friend.' Right now, Dr. Tran wants the contract, but he has a small fleet and wants Dr. Adamson out of the picture. Do you think he can help us? Maybe lead us somewhere?"

"I wouldn't know how he could help us," Danny replied as took a small sip of the wine.

"Aren't these types of data backed up somewhere?"

"The data collected from the field is backed up on tape drives kept in the company's basement. No one is allowed down there besides the tech guys."

"Call and ask to have it retrieved," Valerie said, excitement building in her voice.

"Not a good idea. If we ask to get access, I'll be asked a ton of questions. I can't tell them I need it for Elizabeth's release."

Danny mulled over what Valerie had just said. A few seconds later, a smile stretched across his face.

"What's that smile on your face?" Valerie queried.

"Each ship tracks each other's movements in the ocean during the operation. Dr. Tran should have a copy of our latest data. We can ask him. It was his ship that was trailing Dr. Adamson's ship."

Valerie's eyes lit up. "I'm impressed, detective Maglaya. I guess we'll need to see him tomorrow," she said, walking to the living room.

DANNY FLOPPED HIMSELF ONTO THE loveseat that barely fit into the living room, trying not to think about the daunting task they had to accomplish in the morning.

Valerie walked up to the stereo and placed a CD in the tray. A jazz tune began to play in the background. The mellow sound of trumpet accompanied by a piano softened the tension that had been building between them. Throughout the day, Valerie had been wanting to have a heart-to-heart talk with Danny to find out where they stood. But she couldn't find the opportunity to do so because running away from the two hired killers was nonstop. With this break in the chase, the timing couldn't be more perfect.

WITH ONLY THE LOVESEAT AVAILABLE, he said, "Both of us can fit here."

Valerie gently sat next to him. For the first time after being apart for many months, Danny and Valerie found themselves alone together. As he looked at her, his hunger for her swelled. He wanted her in his arms again and to feel her silky skin with the palm of his hands.

He had been longing for her. He wondered how it would feel to have his hands gliding across her back and down her thighs once again, his lips making gentle landings along the back of her ears and all the way down her shoulder.

The room was quiet except for the syrupy sound of a clarinet.

They said nothing to each other, and the tension grew.

Danny wanted to reach for her hand just a few inches away, but he couldn't muster the courage to do so. He had abandoned Valerie in her grief many months back to try to find the right thing to do. But his absence left a scratch on her heart that would be difficult to erase.

He swirled the wine in his glass. When he looked up, the eyes that he had fallen in love with were directed at him. It was one thing to rationalize and tell themselves to hold back, that the timing wasn't right and they needed more time before getting too intimate again. But in the game of love doing the right thing was never the right thing to do. To do the wrong thing and follow their desire was, for the most part, the only answer to their dilemma. Staying away from each other so they could rid themselves of guilt may be the logical thing to do, but it would only bring more anguish.

She tucked her silky, dark brown hair behind her ear. It flowed seamlessly down her shoulder.

"Let's finish the wine," Danny suggested, reaching for the bottle on the floor, trying to break their suffocating silence.

"Let's split it," Valerie said, lifting her glass. "Fifty-fifty."

Valerie curved her back and bent her left knee, slightly turning to him and exposing the outline of her breasts. Lightness blossomed in his abdomen with him desiring her even more. As they sat together on their loveseat, they watched the orange glow of the fire radiating from the fireplace. Suddenly, as if it was a predetermined act, Danny took the wine glass from her and put it on the table. He moved closer to her, reached for her hand, and pulled her toward him. As he slowly leaned in for a kiss, Valerie met him half-way. Danny didn't hide his pleasure. As her soft lips danced on his own, whatever prelude he had envisioned earlier of easing into knowing her again ended with the desire to be in her arms. He felt an erection between his legs, the tip of his penis slowly rubbing against his inner thighs.

Her tongue swam in his mouth and pleasure rocketed up his spine.

The flame pulsing in the fireplace cast intermittent light across the smooth surface of her arms. The yellow flame glowed, then flickered, adding a soft ambience in the room.

Valerie placed her hand on Danny's side, when all of a sudden he flinched. The area was tender.

"Are you OK?" Valerie asked, taking her hand away. "Let me see."

Danny took his shirt off and turned away from her. Valerie inspected the spot on Danny's side, a few inches from his armpit, and noticed traces of dry, crusted blood around a purple, oval-shaped bruise.

"Is it bad?" Danny asked, remembering how he was slammed against the desk.

"That man must have hit you really hard," Valerie replied.

"I need to take a shower and scrub this off," he said, getting up from the sofa.

Naked, he looked in the mirror. He turned to his side and inspected his back and the side of his torso. There was also a bluish spot on his right hip. Turning to his right, he saw a small gash on his left elbow. He wondered what he should do with Valerie once he finished with his shower. Everything was happening too fast. Just a few hours ago, they were getting shot at and running for their lives. Now, he was alone with the woman he'd always wanted to be with.

He turned the shower knob on and slid into the stall.

The warm water was refreshing as it ran down his chest and arms, soothing his aching muscles. With the tips of his fingers, he massaged his scalp. He looked down and saw a tinge of blood roll down into the drain.

VALERIE HAD BEEN LONGING FOR Danny's caress for months. Their sweet but brief kiss on the couch left her wanting more. She tilted her head back and finished the remaining wine. Deciding that there was no point in trying to take it slow, Valerie tiptoed into the bathroom. She pulled off her blouse. Using her right foot, she pressed on the end of her pant leg to pull it down. Her blue jeans pooled around her feet. She lowered the straps of her bra and unhooked it. She looked at the reflection of her breasts, resembling grapefruits in the mirror as steam formed around it.

As she was taking her panties off, she noticed the two towels hanging on the rack. She had always imagined a house with Danny. There would be two matching towels hanging side by side. Her name would be embroidered on the left towel, and Danny's name would be embroidered on the right. They would never be used, of course, but only there as display—as a reminder that they were lovers.

DANNY HAD JUST FINISHED SOAPING himself when he heard the shower door sliding open. He turned around and saw Valerie standing naked outside the stall. His eyes slowly traced the contours of her body, of her slender arms and curved waist. She offered her hand to him. Danny gently pulled her in. The heat from their bodies and the water warm from the showerhead formed steam on the glass. It felt as if they were floating in the clouds. He leaned on the wall. Hooking his arms around her slender waist, he pressed her body against his. Her wet breasts were soft on his chest.

Danny lovingly stroked her cheek, then began kissing her.

She placed her right hand behind his neck. Her tongue went inside his mouth. Danny slid his hand on the underside of her right upper thigh and slightly lifted her. She moved her kisses along the side of his neck, stopping just above his collarbone, then began swirling her tongue around his Adam's apple. Danny felt a sense of lightness form at the bottom of his head.

Wanting more of her, he placed his hands on her buttocks and pulled her tight against his body. The sound of jazz drifted through the open bathroom door. The drums' crescendo in the living room matched the thumping in his heart. With the cymbals crashing in unison with the water splashing into the tub, his desire for her skyrocketed.

DANNY AND VALERIE EXPLORED EACH other's bodies without restrictions and without shame. As his hands glided all the way down her hips, he felt her nipples harden against his chest, desire burning in their eyes.

He pointed the showerhead down. With her back against the wall, she rested her left foot on the small alcove on the side of the shower and spread her legs.

Overwhelmed with the yearning to make love with her at that very moment, Danny guided himself inside her. Valerie let out a sigh as Danny slid deeper inside. He was pushing her closer to the edge of desire. It felt like both of them were falling into the abyss of passion. She groped the sides of the shower until feeling the door handle. She held it tight. With her other hand, she tightly gripped Danny's wrist. Valerie wanted him to keep going as tremors of ecstasy vibrated through her thighs. Her toes curled and she pushed them down on the floor as the sparks in her lower belly quadrupled. She felt his hard manhood in her opening. The rocking motion was enough to send her to the fifth level of heaven. She threw her arms around his broad shoulders as Danny pushed himself deep inside her once again.

Fourteen

THE SOUND OF SURF POUNDING on the shore woke Danny up. Valerie's arm was draped over his chest and her leg was resting on his thighs. He rubbed his eyes and focused on the clock hanging on the wall, disappointed to see that it was a few minutes before eight. He needed to text Blake at exactly 8:30 a.m. to give him an update. He had to tell Blake what he was planning to prevent him from panicking and calling the police.

He reached for his phone sitting on the nightstand and turned it on. Knowing that it was risky to send his best friend a message, he had no choice.

As soon as he saw Blake's number, he texted, "Call me at exactly 9:00 a.m. I will tell you what I have in mind. Our location is now compromised. I gotta go."

Danny gently shook Valerie. "Wake up, dear. We need to go now."

"BINGO!" IGOR SAID, STARING AT the screen on his laptop.

"You found him?" Yuri asked, drinking vodka straight from the bottle.

"The motherfucker just turned on his phone. He's in Oceanside."

"Oceanside? He has a house there?" Yuri asked, puzzled.

Igor switched to another screen and typed in Danny's information, quickly searching for homes in the area. Though he didn't find a residence listed under Danny's name, he found a woman with the same last name.

"No . . . but I think a relative of his does."

"Search the web and find out who she is. Address, address, I need to know where to go!"

Igor typed the woman's name in the search engine. A social media site popped up. There in broad daylight, Danny was standing next to her with several of his family members. Opening another window, he typed the woman's full name on a realtor website.

"I know exactly where it is," Igor said, closing his laptop.

YURI COCKED HIS WEAPON. AT a slow, calculated pace, he quietly approached the front door of the cottage and placed a sound level meter against the wall of the house, trying to detect any conversation. When the needle didn't flinch, he pressed his ear against the door himself. Danny or

Valerie could already have detected their arrival and might put up a fight as soon as he barged through the front door. Not knowing what weapon Danny might have, he texted Igor who was standing on the side of the house, instructing him to go to the rear door and enter simultaneously for the element of surprise.

Yuri adjusted his bulletproof vest. Knowing that the only way to find out for sure if Danny and Valerie were inside, he texted Igor again to pull his weapon out and ready himself for the kill.

Seeing that Igor was ready for action, Yuri pointed to the house and mouthed, "I'm going in."

Wasting no more time, Yuri kicked the front door. It flew open. Igor barged through the back door at the same time. Gripping his pistol tightly in his hands, slightly hunched, he aimed in front of him, sweeping side-to-side and ready to shoot. He found no one in the living room. He rushed to the bedroom, only to find the pillows neatly arranged at the head of the bed.

Igor pushed the bathroom door, surprised to see that it was empty with only the sound of the water dripping from the faucet.

The cottage was empty.

DANNY LOWERED THE KICKSTAND WITH his foot and parked the motorcycle. Sitting on the curb in front of residential houses on the hill above the airport, he watched jumbo jets land at the nearby San Diego International Airport.

From his vantage point, he could see the large hangars along the Pacific Coast Highway. At one time they were the primary manufacturing plant that made B-24s in World War II.

Earlier, in his text to Blake, he told him about the incident that happened during the chase, but didn't elaborate, aware that his phone was monitored and their location was being triangulated. Danny was certain that Blake would be distraught about the bad news, but he was confident that after providing his solution, Blake's worries would be erased. He cryptically asked Blake how he could get ahold of Dr. Tran.

As Danny waited for Blake's call, he marveled at the construction below in downtown San Diego that looked like pieces of toy blocks. It was almost 9:00 a.m. The sea of vehicles going northbound on the Interstate 5 swished past, creating a droning sound. The cars were like tiny toys racing through the freeway eager to get to their destinations. Many of them would go home to their loved ones with a kiss, and not a gun aimed at their head. He wondered how he could get themselves out of the jam they were in.

Valerie swung her legs around the motorcycle and leaned on the seat. Taking her helmet off, her hair cascaded down her back, covering the side of her face. She raked it with her fingers and tucked it behind her ear. She turned to Danny as he nervously fidgeted with his phone. Blake would be calling him any second. He worried that when they met with Dr. Tran, the professor wouldn't have the data that his ship had gathered from his 30-day sea experiments—or worse, he wouldn't want to share it in the first place. If that happened, Blake would likely never see his fiancée again.

VALERIE MOVED CLOSER TO DANNY. Resting her head on his chest and being close to him was the only comfort she could have for the moment. She watched the marine layer curling over the ocean, blanketing the tip of Point Loma to the north and shrouding the skyline along the waterfront. She was confident that the rising sun would heat up the land, burn off the fog, and reveal the pristine coastline. Like the doubt she had that might lift as soon as they arranged a meeting with Dr. Tran.

A JUMBO JET HAD JUST touched down on the black stained runway when Danny felt his phone vibrate. Blake's picture appeared on the screen.

Danny pressed the phone to his ear and answered. "Blake!"

"What really happened?"

"I'm sorry for losing the thumb drive," Danny responded.

There was silence at the other end of the phone. Danny could tell that his best friend was disappointed.

"Were they able to take it away from you?"

"No. It flew under the car. It was in Valerie's clutch bag and fell on the freeway."

"Do you think Dr. Adamson might already have it?"

"No. I saw the car burning from the side mirror. I think it was destroyed. It's a long story."

"Do you know where I can find the professor who helped us design the grid for moving fish from different sections in the ocean?" Danny said, sounding cryptic. "I need to get to him. Don't mention his name."

"Why do you need to find him?"

"Valerie and I came up with a possible solution. I can't tell you now, but if we're successful, I'll tell you where to meet next. I'll talk to you in five hours."

"Go to the restaurant his brother owns. You know the place, right?"

"Yes," Danny responded, sounding confident.

"OK . . . five hours. After that, I'm calling the police," Blake said resolutely. "I hope you understand. Check her latest picture."

Danny pressed the mail button on his phone. As soon as he opened the attachment, Elizabeth's picture filled the entire screen. The water line had already reached all the way up to her navel. The petrified look on her face was a punch to his gut

"I'm really sorry," Danny replied. "I'll get this done right away."

AFTER GETTING ON THE OFF-RAMP of the 163 freeway, Danny and Valerie arrived in Linda Vista. The community had been a favorite neighborhood to many Vietnamese immigrants who fled their country after the fall of Saigon in 1975.

The Vietnamese restaurant had been owned by Dr. Tran's family since the late eighties. Danny remembered Dr. Tran telling him that it was because of the restaurant that he and his siblings were able to attend graduate school. Walking past tables filled with patrons enjoying *pho*—beef soup with rice noodles, Danny could smell the strong aromas of fish sauce and basil as he hurried straight to the counter.

Danny recognized Dr. Tran's brother, Duc, as he was pushing the cash register drawer closed. Danny had been in the restaurant a few times when he and Blake had met with Dr. Tran, so Duc knew him pretty well.

"Danny! You here for lunch?"

"Duc, happy to see you. We're looking for the professor," Danny said politely.

Duc smiled at him and replied, "He not here. Isn't he in the lab?"

"No. Do you know where he is?"

"His house . . . did you call?"

"We don't know the number."

"Where can we find him?" Valerie added. "It's an urgent matter."

Duc drummed his fingers on the counter thinking where he could locate his brother. He unclipped his cell phone from his belt, and dialed a number.

"He not answering his phone. When he doesn't answer, he wants to be left alone. Maybe stressed from work. He goes on a retreat at his house in Borrego Desert."

Danny had heard the professor commenting about going to a secluded location to reset his brain and take a breather from the lab and from teaching at the university. The ranch house was in the middle of the desert with a private airstrip.

It would take them at least two hours to get there by motorcycle, and they would be wasting a lot of time. The only option to get there fast was to fly.

FIFTEEN

DANNY COULD STILL VIVIDLY REMEMBER that afternoon when he first took his solo flight in a Cessna 152 at Montgomery Field, where he and Valerie had just arrived. If saving the world's fish population was Danny's calling, flying airplanes was his passion. If he wasn't on the boat conducting research, he could be found strapped in the cockpit of his Ryan PT-22, flying through the sky at 10,000 feet.

With their hands on its yellow wings, Danny and Valerie pushed the airplane out of the hangar and onto the taxiway. It had been built in the 1930s, as a trainer for the U.S. Army Air Corps. The aluminum fuselage gleamed in the late morning sun. He had bought the plane from his fellow scientists and flew it regularly when he had the luxury to take a day off from work. After spending long hours in the lab, flying never failed to rid his mind of the stress of work. He assisted Valerie into the front seat and strapped her in. She wrapped a white scarf around her neck and slipped a leather helmet on. She strapped goggles to her face and plugged in the headset.

Danny jumped in the cockpit behind Valerie. After turning on the electrical units, he spoke into the microphone. "Can you hear me OK?"

"Ten-four."

Danny kicked the rudder, testing if it moved freely. He pushed the control stick forward then back, the elevators reacting up and down. He then pushed the stick left, and the aileron on the left wing went up.

He scanned his surroundings, making sure no one was near the plane.

"Clear!"

He clicked the ignition and the propellers started spinning. The wind blew back in their faces. Looking left and right, Danny checked for cross traffic making sure that the path was clear as they slowly taxied to the runway.

Sitting at the runway, Danny anxiously waited for the tower to give clearance for takeoff. He thought of Charles Lindbergh in 1927 when he picked up the single engine airplane called Spirit of St. Louis after it was built a few miles away by the same company who also manufactured the plane he was piloting. Did the famous aviator feel the same trepidation as Danny before he took off for New York? The starting point for his nonstop transatlantic flight.

He took a quick peek at the back of Valerie's head, wondering if she was just as nervous as he was on how the day might turn out.

About a minute later, he heard the air traffic controller's instructions for departure. They were finally cleared for takeoff.

Danny pushed the throttle forward. The engine responded with a loud choppy sound.

As they rolled down the runway, the airplane became faster with each passing second. Seeing that they had reached the takeoff speed on the cockpit panel, he pulled the control stick back. The airplane's nose tilted up. The dashed white line in the middle of the runway below them smeared along with black tire marks. Steadily, the plane lifted away from the ground beneath them. The end of the runway receded like a fading memory. They were getting closer to the blue sky.

The outline of the horizon appeared on the tip of the airplane's nose, Danny looked down at his first checkpoint—Mount Soledad. It was hard to fathom that it was just yesterday that he was staring directly into his killer's eyes, wondering if he would be captured alive or killed in a fiery motorcycle crash.

He banked the airplane to the right, heading north and following the coastline. To his right were roads curving like capillaries, outlined with houses and green patches of lawn. Adding more power, the wooden propeller bit more air. The wings flexed; he felt a slight drop.

VALERIE LOOKED DOWN AT THE red tiled rooftops along the hillsides and thought of the houses she had designed while working as an architect. When she and Danny were dating, she had dreamed of owning a home with a view of the ocean. It would be the domicile where she would play the part of his lovely wife, and he would always be at her side as her friend and lover.

Valerie could still vividly remember that Sunday afternoon when Danny came to her apartment. She was going to show him the blueprint of a house she had just designed. Though it was a paid commission by a client—a house with a red sloping tile roof, a blue kidney-shaped swimming pool, a green backyard, and a white picket fence—she was hoping Danny would get the message and get serious with her. But instead, that day became one of the worst days in her life. Danny told her that he wanted to cool their relationship and stay friends for the moment; he needed to work out the guilt that he felt for falling in love with someone other than Helen. She was devastated.

She pushed her thoughts aside and tried to distract herself with the sight of docile hot air balloons floating off the ground.

Reaching the city of Del Mar, they flew over the racetrack, steering clear of the cotton-like clouds. Danny turned northeast and headed straight toward the Borrego Desert.

ABOUT A HALF HOUR LATER, the plane flew over the mountains. The dips and valleys of the desert came into view. The reddish surface of the earth was scored below him. The irregularly shaped, treeless mountains with finger-like foothills crawling into the flattening desert floor had an ominous appearance as if they were formidable walls to fly over.

"We'll be descending soon. You OK up there?" Danny asked, speaking through the microphone attached to his headset.

"I'm fine here. Are we almost there?" Valerie replied, the noise from the wind and the propeller blades making it hard for her to hear.

"About twenty minutes more."

The topography soon changed to a dry brown landscape as soon as he passed the rugged mountains. Danny pulled the throttle back, and the airplane began its slow descent. Boulders were scattered along the sides of the mountains. He could see the plane's shadow gliding along the barren desert floor. He followed the straight line of a two-lane dirt road disappearing in the horizon. A lone car was speeding by, tossing a plume of dry desert dust behind.

He checked his GPS. His destination was just minutes away.

He banked the airplane to the right for a better view. He was glad to see Dr. Tran's private airstrip at two o'clock.

Preparing to land, he estimated their distance from the ground, then aligned the aircraft with the runway strip. He cut the power and the engine idled. The specks of green brush magnified as they got closer to the parched land. As the aircraft eased down onto the runway, he pulled the control stick back and a cushion of air softened the landing.

DANNY KNOCKED ON THE FRONT door several times, then silently waited. Valerie shot a glance at him while nervously twirling a piece of hair dangling on the side of her face. Noticing her unease, he reached for her hand and gently squeezed it to calm her down.

"It's going to be fine," Danny whispered.

"Do you think he can help us?"

"He hates Dr. Adamson's guts. Of course, he will," Danny answered with conviction.

A few minutes later, Danny heard soft footsteps coming from the other side of the door. He straightened his body and clutched the laptop tighter in his hand. When the door opened, Dr. Tran was standing in front of them with a shocked expression on his face. He wore a blue button-down shirt over white pants, looking very comfortable in his outfit.

"Danny, what a surprise!" Dr. Tran said.

"I'm sorry to just barge in without advance notice. We were trying to call you, but you weren't answering."

Dr. Tran, sensing the urgency in Danny's voice, replied, "Why don't you come in?"

The professor disappeared into the kitchen while Danny and Valerie waited in the large living room, furnished with several burgundy-colored couches and a large Chinese vase in each corner.

When Dr. Tran returned, he was carrying a tray with three cups of rooibos tea, with cream and sugar on the side.

"I recently discovered this tea, and I liked it," Dr. Tran said, placing it on the coffee table.

"It's like hibiscus tea," Valerie replied, reaching for one of the cups.

"Dr. Tran, without getting you involved and going into too much detail, do you remember the exact place where Blake told you that we had found the breakthrough with the Rx-18 compound and that we were going operational?"

"Of course, how could I not? I've been anticipating its result for years. From what I remember, I met with Blake at Balboa Park. He discussed your invention in detail."

"Do you remember where in the park exactly?"

Dr. Tran placed his fingers under his chin and turned toward the large glass window, a view of the desert stretching on for miles.

"I really don't understand why you're asking me all this. I have a feeling we're talking cryptically here. Is there something I should know? Are you in trouble with the law? If you're not straight with me, then how can I help you?"

Sensing Dr. Tran's rising tension in his voice, Valerie intervened. "Pardon us if we sound jittery, but we're in a bit of jam. Blake's fiancée was kidnapped, and the kidnappers are demanding that we upload the data from the Rx-18 compound's sea experiment results for her release or she will be killed."

"Then why are you asking me where I met with Blake?"

"Two men are chasing us, trying to stop us from uploading the information. Our phones were hacked, and they're watching our every move."

"You are in a very tough situation," Dr. Tran said, stroking the wisps of hair sticking out of his chin.

"This is the only way we could meet without being discovered," Danny reiterated.

"From what I can remember, I was leading a tour of middle-school students at the Museum of Man. Right after I finished, Blake arrived, and I took him to the top of the California Tower."

"Thank you," Valerie replied.

"But I don't think that's the only reason you came here," Dr. Tran asked, cutting to the chase. "Please just tell me."

"Our hard drives were attacked and wiped clean. The data on the thumb drive was the only copy. I was hoping you can help us?"

"I'm assuming you came here hoping I have a copy?" Dr. Tran asked, his eyes narrowing. "I only have a copy of the data we gathered."

"I have Dr. Adamson's data on the laptop's hard drive. Your data and his would be sufficient. I can remotely access the data from the other ship through my home server. Dr. Adamson hasn't attacked it yet."

"How will you do that?"

"If you let me copy your raw data, I can superimpose it with what's on the laptop, render it, and come up with the exact same analyzed data that was on the thumb drive. I'll use that. The kidnappers won't know the difference even if they did their analysis."

Dr. Tran's face contorted into a look of panic. From where Danny sat, he could tell that the man was distressed by the news. Dr. Tran got up from the couch and walked to the master bedroom.

"I don't think he has what we need. His lab is about a hundred miles away," Valerie said, sounding concerned.

"He is our only option."

"I think Blake is right. We need to call the police while we still have time."

"There's nothing they can do. No one knows where Elizabeth is being held."

Valerie was about to make another point when she heard Dr. Tran's footsteps coming from the bedroom.

"I just called one of my guys at my lab. It's being sent to my phone as we speak."

Danny pressed the laptop's power button. With its solid-state technology, it came on instantly. He went to settings and activated the "near-field communication" feature. After the computer and Dr. Tran's phone had recognized each other, he downloaded the email attachment. He logged onto his personal server, glad to see that the data still hadn't been wiped out. Comparing the raw data feeds from all the ships at sea, he wasted no time putting them together. Fifteen minutes later, the data was compiled and the graphics showed the ships' movement.

"It all looks good," Danny said, turning to Dr. Tran.

Dr. Tran opened his hand and said, "I think you might need this."

Danny saw a thumb drive in the center of the professor's palm.

"Thank you."

"It's the same class of thumb drive you lost. The dedicated laptop Blake is carrying shouldn't have any problem reading it," Dr. Tran said.

Danny transferred the data to the thumb drive.

Satisfied that they had accomplished what they set out to do, Danny and Valerie got up from the couch and headed for the front door.

"We must be going now," Danny said, reaching for the door handle. "Thank you for your help. I don't know how to repay your kindness."

"You already have more than you know," Dr. Tran responded with an enigmatic smile.

THROUGH THE LARGE WINDOW, DR. Tran watched the nose of the WWII-era airplane pitch up. He patiently waited as the Ryan PT-22 slowly climbed as it headed west. Not more than five minutes had elapsed when the plane had become just a speck in the blue sky, he drew the curtain and walked back to his study. He flopped himself into his chair, feeling frustrated, then pressed a speed dial on his phone. A few rings later, a baritone voice answered, "I thought there was no communication until tomorrow."

"We have a big problem. Dr. Adamson hired two goons to stop Danny and Blake from uploading the data to the server."

"How do you know that?" the calm voice on the other end asked.

"Danny was just here with his lady friend. Send one of your guys and protect him until the data is uploaded and the task is completed," Dr. Tran said with authority in his voice.

"How will I find him?"

"There is a tracking device on the thumb drive I just gave him. I'm texting you the identification number right now."

"We'll do our best," the calm voice replied.

"I'm not paying you to do your best. I'm paying you to get the job done. He must rendezvous with Blake. It is vital that they upload the data, or we will be in deep shit!"

Sixteen

About five miles out, the topography changed from the tumbleweed-dotted desert to the lush greenery of tall trees and apple orchards. The town of Julian, famous in its heyday as a destination for gold mining was straight ahead. It was just three months ago that Danny and Valerie had been walking its crowded streets, holding hands as the delicious smell of fresh apple pies filled the air.

The Ryan PT-22 had just flown back over the sharp mountain range when, from out of nowhere, a helicopter appeared in the sun's direction, about a football field away from them on the right. If it wasn't for the way it was closing in on them in a straight line, he wouldn't have thought anything of it. But as the double-bladed chopper flew closer, he knew that trouble was on the way. He reached for the throttle and pushed forward. The engine drank more fuel as it struggled to turn the propeller. The needle on the airspeed indicator slowly made its way further to the right, but the 65-year-old aircraft couldn't go any faster than 125 miles per hour. Outrunning the chopper would be impossible.

"Tighten your seatbelt. We have company," Danny said over the intercom.

Danny looked behind him. To his shock, he saw the helicopter gaining on them. Manufactured as just a trainer, their plane wasn't as agile as the modernized helicopter. He wished he was flying a fighter aircraft like the P-51 Mustang. His problem would have been solved with its four-bladed propeller powered by a Merlin engine.

WHEN THE HELICOPTER WAS WITHIN striking range, a man sitting inside its open door aimed his AR-15 at them and pulled the trigger. The assault weapon spat smoldering slugs intended to tear through the aircraft's thin fuselage. Danny banked the airplane left and kicked the rudder pedal, dodging the bullets. The airplane pulled away from the copter.

THE MAN REPOSITIONED HIS AIM and started shooting again. Half of the shells dropped on the floor, and the other half fell 3,000 feet down below.

"HANG ON!" DANNY SHOUTED OVER the intercom.

There were a few seconds when the shooting stopped.

Danny knew that the gunner was reloading and that the next time the gunner took aim, he and Valerie could end up at the bottom of the valley.

He looked down for an escape. He pulled the throttle back and banked the airplane to the left, losing several hundred feet in altitude. Flying low through the trees was his only alternative. He could fly close to the mountain, hoping the helicopter pilot would make a poor judgment and crash into one of the tall pines. Danny pushed the control stick forward. The airplane quickly responded and the nose pointed down.

But the helicopter continued its dogged pursuit.

Danny scratched the idea right away. Instead, he aimed the plane directly into sagging power lines suspended from their towers—into at least 700,000 volts of electricity.

"This is going to be close!" This time distress cutting in his voice.

"Watch out for the tower!" Valerie shouted back.

Danny slowed down, luring the helicopter to get closer.

The helicopter pilot was unperturbed and steadily followed Danny. The gunner aimed his automatic rifle back at the plane and pulled the trigger. Bullets exited the muzzle of the automatic rifle and arched down to puncture the Ryan PT-22.

Just as he was about to run into the electrical wires, Danny pushed the stick forward. The aircraft dipped underneath, just missing them. Several bullets hit the engine, busting one of the pistons. The engine began to sputter as if it was its dying breath. Smoke puffed from the nose cowling and oil streaked from the plane, trailing over its canary yellow wings.

As soon as Danny cleared the hanging cable, he pulled back on the stick. Though the engine was already losing precious fluids, the plane's momentum gave enough energy to push the aircraft another fifty feet back up into the sky.

THE HELICOPTER PILOT, NOT WANTING to lose Danny, pulled up after him. Just as he was about to pass under the power lines, he increased the main rotor spin and pulled up. But he miscalculated the ascent, hurrying to get Danny within firing range. The tail rotor clipped one of the transmission tower's arms. The helicopter's nose violently pitched up. Sparks exploded from the tail boom. The main rotor blade broke off. Like a dragonfly caught in a spider's web, it lost lift. The two-ton chopper came crashing down into the canyon, dropping like a bag full of sand.

DANNY SAW THE HELICOPTER TUMBLING down, glad that the threat was eliminated. To avoid being electrocuted by the dangling cable, he kicked full right rudder. The airplane did not respond. Fear erupted at the bottom of his stomach. He suspected that the bullets had severed the lines connected to the rudder because he could no longer control the plane's longitudinal axis. They were going to crash into the trees.

Seeing a two-lane road up ahead, his hopes lifted. It was a good enough place to set the airplane down. He pulled the throttle back and the engine idled. He aligned the nose along the dashed highway lines, using the ailerons to bank left and right. With his decreasing speed, the thickening smoke from the burning oil blocked his vision. It became difficult to estimate his distance from the ground. With the engine in its last gasp, Danny had only one chance to land the plane properly. If he failed his approach, he wouldn't have enough power to make a go-around—he'd crash into the side of the mountain.

The airplane touched down, bouncing several times on the black asphalt road. He slammed on the brakes with the tips of his toes. To his horror, the airplane kept rolling forward and wouldn't stop. The brake lines were also severed. Emerald green trees blurred past him. There wasn't any way for him to stop their forward momentum.

"Brace yourself!" Danny shouted through the intercom.

The airplane swerved to the shoulder until the front hit a large rock protruding out of the ground. Their forward momentum was stopped, preventing them from sliding all the way down the slope at the side of the road.

Danny unbuckled himself and dropped to the ground. He hurried to Valerie's aid, reached for the safety harness and released it.

"You OK?"

"Just a little bruised," Valerie said, yanking the goggles off her face.

"We need to get away from here. Someone probably saw us and already called 9-1-1," Danny said, taking off his leather jacket and helmet. "Help me push this thing so no one can see it."

With all the strength Danny and Valerie could muster, they pushed the plane down the embankment.

No MORE THAN TWENTY MINUTES had passed when an old blue pickup truck stopped in front of them.

"We're going to Julian," Danny said, peering into the passenger-side window noticing stacks of egg crates sitting on the front passenger seat.

"That's where I'm going, but you're gonna have to sit on the truck bed, if that's OK with you," an old Caucasian male in a blue coverall said.

The driver stepped on the gas and soon they were bumping along the road.

Danny checked his watch. It was now 3:00 p.m. They had four hours, plenty of time to get to Balboa Park. Danny was overcome with relief. They would be able to make it on time to meet with Blake. Elizabeth would be freed. With that thought his mind relaxed.

Danny reached for his phone and texted Blake. "Meet you at the same spot where you had your last meeting with the Professor. I'll text you half hour before I get there."

Sending a message was a risky move but he had no other choice. He had to tell Blake what was going on.

A few seconds later, Danny received a text back from Blake. "On my way."

Danny shut his phone, stretched his legs, and leaned against the back of the pickup cab. The tall posts with electrical wires appeared and reappeared lining the side of the road.

The wind swirled wildly in the back of the truck. Valerie's hair fluttered in her face. She tied her hair into a ponytail with a rubber band she picked up off the floor then hooked one arm behind Danny and rested the other one on his stomach.

THE DRIVER DROPPED THEM OFF on Main Street, right in the heart of Julian. Danny jumped out of the truck, worried about not knowing how to get back to San Diego. He turned around and offered his hand to Valerie to assist her down.

"Thank you," Danny said, tapping the back of the truck several times. The driver waved goodbye and sped off.

"There's a bunch of people heading back to San Diego. Maybe we could ask one of them to give us a ride?" Valerie suggested.

"Too risky. People are too suspicious nowadays. Someone might call the police."

"But we need to get out of here fast."

He set his sights across the street. There was a line of people waiting beneath a sign that read, "The Best Apple Pie and Cider in Town."

Not knowing who to call, Danny fished Pradeep's calling card from his wallet. Tapping the card several times on his thumbnail, he looked for somewhere to make the call. Using a landline was his only option to avoid detection. There were various stores along Main Street: a general store, a soap store, a bakery, a deli, a gift shop and a boutique.

"Let's go into the general store and ask the owner if we can use the phone," Danny said.

Danny and Valerie were about to cross the street when a black SUV drove past them. Suspicious, Danny shot a glance at the ominous vehicle. To his horror, he saw the bald man, his snakehead tattoo protruding out of his shirt collar. Danny looked away to avoid eye contact, but it was too late. Just at that moment, he saw Igor turning in his direction.

"We need to go now!" Danny shouted.

THE SUV CAME TO A screeching halt in the middle of Main Street. The passenger door flew open and Igor bolted out, heading straight for Danny and Valerie.

"THERE!" VALERIE YELLED, POINTING TO an alley between a candy shop and a candle store. Nearby were tourists sitting on benches with ice cream cones in their hands. "We can blend in with the crowd."

Although stealing a car was the last thing he wanted to do, it was his only option if he wanted to live another day.

"Hurry . . . this way!" Danny directed as he led her to the backstreets.

Several cars lined the roads. Danny searched for an old car that would be easier to hot-wire—newer cars have a preprogrammed chip in their keys and would be impossible to steal.

A car stopped a few feet in front of them. The driver, a young man who looked no older than 19 years old, opened the door and ran into the deli. To Danny's delight, the engine was still running.

"Let's get in," Danny blurted out.

He was about to jump into the driver's seat when he felt massive hands grasp his shoulders. Danny pivoted and swiped the hands away from him. He found himself face to face with Igor, sweat dripping down his temples, the stench of tobacco flowing from his mouth.

The bald man swung at him.

Danny turned away to avoid getting hit in the face, but Igor landed a punch on the side of his torso. The pain shot through his ribcage.

Seeing Danny clutching his side just above his kidney, Igor pulled out a switchblade from his boot to finish Danny off.

Waving the knife with a menacing smile, he leaped at Danny.

Danny jumped out of the way. The blade chipped green paint off the top of the car.

Danny grabbed Igor's arm and with lightning speed slammed the side of his left hand into his opponent's wrist. The knife fell out of Igor's hand and tumbled to the ground.

Not giving up easily, Igor followed up with a hard push. Danny was thrown back and fell to the ground.

Igor bent down and picked up the knife. With a quick forward step, he jumped on top of Danny. He raised the switchblade over his head and aimed it at Danny's chest, intending to rip his heart out. As Igor plunged the sharp blade, Danny turned to his side and drove his right knee directly into Igor's stomach, throwing the man off balance. The blade missed Danny by mere inches, the knife smashing into the concrete sidewalk.

Igor began swinging his fists wildly. Danny crossed his arms in front of his eyes, blocking any blows that might land on his face. Then, exploiting Igor's miscalculations, Danny threw a quick uppercut.

Igor flew back and fell on the hard concrete.

"In the car now!" Danny yelled, getting up quickly.

As Danny sprinted towards the driver-side door, Igor scrambled to reach Danny.

The getaway car was close, but Igor was in the way; it was impossible to get in.

Finishing off this animal was the only way he could save himself and Valerie from getting killed. He had to take care of business and finish their dilemma once and for all. It was a fight to the death. In a few minutes, one of them would be left standing, while the other would be lying on the ground with a stab wound.

Igor sliced left and right. Almost lacerating Danny's muscular biceps, the knife caught his shirt and cut the skin just below his armpit. Bright red blood oozed out of the opening.

With renewed confidence, Igor galloped forward, intending to plunge the knife into him.

Danny sidestepped quickly to get out of the way and grabbed Igor's hand, holding the knife with both of his hands.

Igor pushed him until Danny's back slammed against the side of the car. Igor thrust the knife, leaning in with his entire body weight, aiming for Danny's throat. Danny winced in pain as the searing heat radiated from where he had just been cut.

Igor grunted as he aimed for the kill. Danny's muscles weakened with each passing second. He needed to do something fast or he might not see the end of the day. The only way he could escape was to get the weapon away from the bald man in front of him. But it was too difficult. Igor was too heavy with all his weight pushing down on him. Danny couldn't nudge the animal even a centimeter. Danny's strength was dwindling as Igor's strength was picking up momentum.

Danny resisted the insurmountable force bearing down on him, but he could feel his arms getting weaker. The pain of holding back was too much to take. His vision began to blur in the corners. He was running out of energy to resist Igor.

Just as the tip of the knife was about to slice through his Adam's apple, Danny drew on the final ounce of his strength, knowing he could be dead in a few seconds, and forced the knife away from him. The knife smashed into the driver side window. He followed up with a hard elbow into Igor's neck.

Igor head-butted Danny.

The searing pain detonated in his forehead. Seconds later, the spot turned red. The pain spread throughout his brain. The impact jarred Danny, but he regained his composure right away. He advanced. With both hands, he grabbed Igor's shirt and with all the energy he could summon from his exhausted body, he shoved his knee into his enemy's groin. Igor tilted forward in pain. Danny drew back his arm for maximum effect and punched Igor in the face. He felt his opponent's cheekbone shatter beneath his knuckles.

Danny picked up the switchblade from the ground. Flexing his arm, Danny raised the knife over his head. He was ready to follow up with the same amount of force and retaliation. This time, Danny had no qualms about killing him.

Danny was about to plunge the knife into Igor's chest, to finish him off for good, when he heard Valerie's shriek.

"Danny!"

From the tone of her voice, Danny knew that it was not good. He turned around and saw the terror on Valerie's face.

"Drop it or I'll put a bullet in her brain," a man with a mullet haircut commanded, holding a gun to the back of her head.

Danny looked back at Igor who was getting up.

"OK . . . please don't hurt her," Danny replied, setting the knife on the ground.

Igor walked up to Danny and kicked the knife away from him, then backhanded him. Danny was powerless to do anything. The murderous intent was evident in his adversary's eyes and could not be mistaken, his facial expression coagulating in total hate.

Danny stood helpless and defeated. The man flashed a maniacal grin and reached for the 9mm that the man with a mullet handed him. Danny knew it was going to be his end. Igor aimed the cocked pistol directly at his head. He was going to die in a few seconds, and there wasn't anything he could do. He glanced at Valerie standing just a few feet away from him, helpless. So, this was where he was going to die, he thought to himself—on the streets of Julian.

Igor was about to pull the trigger and finish Danny off when his phone rang. He cursed under his breath. With reluctance, Igor answered the call. Though Danny couldn't understand what he was saying, the bald man didn't look happy. Danny scanned the sky and saw a drone flying overhead, exposing how Igor and his associates had been able to track them down so quickly.

Igor took out a plastic zip tie from his pocket and threw it at the man holding Valerie.

"Tie her up. The boss wants them alive."

Igor grabbed Danny's hands and bound them.

"I kill you later. I promise. I do it slow," Igor said, groping for the thumb drive in Danny's front pocket.

Igor spat on the ground next to Danny's foot and shoved him inside the black SUV.

DANNY WAS SITTING IN THE rear seat when the man with the mullet opened the back passenger door and threw Valerie inside like a rag doll, flopping her on the seat next to Danny. Her hair was disheveled, tears rolling down her cheeks.

"It's OK. We'll be OK," Danny said, trying to comfort Valerie.

The vehicle rolled away. Danny wanted to shout for help. Since the incident occurred on Julian's backstreets and no one saw the fight, he knew his efforts would be fruitless. Through closed dark tinted windows, he watched families spending a pleasant afternoon together, clueless to their plight. Not a single soul in Julian was aware that Danny and Valerie had just been abducted.

"You not so smart after all using your phone," Igor said with victory in his voice.

"I had no choice," Danny replied.

"Thank you for being stupid and making my job a lot easier. You could have at least thrown your phone away and bought a new one so we couldn't track you."

"It wouldn't have made any difference. You are monitoring all the incoming voice and text messages between Blake and me."

"Now that you say that, I take it back, you're smarter than I thought. But it does not matter now because it looks like you are fucked," Igor said with an irritating laugh.

"Why are you doing this to us?"

"I get paid to do a job. It's what I do. But because I'm nice, I'll tell you anyway. Dr. Adamson wants you alive for now so we can trap Blake. Don't know why. Just an hour ago, he wanted you dead. I guess it's easier to get you both," Igor responded.

"And why would I cooperate with you?" Danny asked, exasperated.

"Easy . . . I kill your girlfriend if you don't," Igor answered, moving his eyes off Danny and back onto the road in front of him.

It was quiet in the car. Valerie sat next to Danny, trying to wiggle her hands free from the zip tie around her wrists. Danny thought of choking out Igor, sitting in the front passenger seat, with his two bound hands. It could work, but if things went awry and Igor reached for his gun and started shooting, he or Valerie could get killed.

Danny looked outside. He knew that they had been driving south on Highway 79 and had turned west on Interstate 8. From what he could discern from his surroundings, they were somewhere in the city of Alpine.

The rooftops of the nearby neighborhood began appearing in the distance, in between the tall pine trees on the side of the freeway. At the edge of the shoulder, Danny saw a large green exit sign. Workers in orange safety hats and vests were walking in a single file line, collecting trash along the freeway as their supervisor watched them like a hawk.

Through his left window, Danny noticed a white SUV pulling up beside them. Both vehicles were approaching the overpass. The passenger-side window of the white SUV rolled down and the long barrel of a rifle jutted out. He grabbed the overhead handle and braced himself.

"Valerie . . . hang on!"

As soon as he lowered his head and closed his eyes, the driver-side window shattered. Pieces of glass flew all over the cabin. There were nonstop popping sounds until the left rear tire came apart. The vehicle began fishtailing. The driver tried to maintain a steady course, but with the sudden loss of traction in the back of the SUV, they violently spun from side to side. Danny held on, feeling his stomach tighten as he feared for his life. The centrifugal force threw the SUV to the side of the freeway, somersaulting into a pine tree, then landing upside down, teeter-tottering on its roof. Danny could feel his seatbelt pressing against his chest, holding him suspended and keeping him from smashing his face on the windshield. He looked to his right. Valerie was upside down too, hanging from her seatbelt as her hair cascaded down.

"Get out now!" Danny shouted.

"I can't get this thing off me!" Valerie exclaimed, trying to wiggle out of her seatbelt.

Danny checked the inside of the car for a knife to cut them loose. He noticed that the driver had been thrown out of the vehicle, laying by the road with blood and dirt all over his body. Danny could see Igor was tucked in the nook between the dashboard and the windshield, his chest rising and falling, with what looked like a broken leg.

Danny pressed the seatbelt's release button, dropping to his knees and stomach. Once he was freed, he faced Valerie. Reaching around her back, he unbuckled her right away.

Smelling gasoline leaking from the tank, he said, "This thing will go up in flames any minute now!"

Valerie frantically crawled out.

Just as he was about to exit, he felt a large hand gripping his left calf. Danny kicked back and felt Igor's face on the bottom of his foot. He almost forgot that Igor still had the thumb drive. With smoke from the engine filling inside the SUV, Danny knew that it could burn anytime. Danny turned around. Igor was looking at him as if pleading to get rescued. Danny thought of saving the man and pulling him out.

But Igor did the unthinkable. He grabbed Danny's throat attempting to choke him, but there was no strength in his grip. Danny grabbed his wrist and pulled it away from him.

Danny realized that if he saved Igor, his life would be in jeopardy and the paid assassin would try again to complete his mission. Danny reached inside Igor's pocket. Feeling the hard plastic case with the tips of his fingers, he retrieved the thumb drive and backed away from his injured nemesis.

As they ran from the scene of the crash, Danny heard a crackling sound. He looked back just in time to see fire coming out of the back of the vehicle. A second later, the deafening sound of an explosion filled the quiet afternoon air.

The black SUV was engulfed in fire along with the man who wanted him dead.

Since there was nothing but a couple of gas stations on the north side of the freeway, Danny and Valerie were out in the open. He searched the immediate area for the any signs of the white SUV. He wondered if Dr. Adamson sent a second team to end the chase and finish him for good. But just as it appeared out of nowhere, it disappeared like a bubble.

Getting to the other side of the freeway was critical. There was a strip mall where they could blend in with shoppers without looking suspicious. As they were running across the overpass, Danny saw the cars heading westbound had stopped, stuck behind the debris of car parts littering the highway.

Danny and Valerie sprinted across the on-ramp through the narrow strip between the white line and the guardrail. The cars passing by swished wind in their face. Finally making it to the other side, with Danny leading the way, they walked across a patch of dirt covered with brown weeds and thorny bushes. They walked under a traffic light on the corner and passed by the highway entrance sign.

They had just entered the strip mall when the sound of a siren blaring in the distance caught their attention. A fire truck was speeding to the scene, warning the cars in front of it to get out of the way.

"Here . . . now," Danny said, directing Valerie to hide behind a restaurant.

Danny and Valerie flattened their backs against the wall and looked away as two police cruisers and an ambulance zipped past them.

As soon as it was clear, they moved away from the wall and searched for a place to make a phone call.

From where he stood, Danny could see the tall black smoke billowing across the freeway. He wondered if the bald-headed man with the snake tattoo was already dead. A part of him wished he had pulled him to safety but he didn't have any choice. The animal was intent on killing him. Leaving him pinned between the dashboard and the windshield to die was his only option.

Danny looked around the parking area for someone who might give them a ride to Balboa Park. A tow truck occupying two spaces was parked near a tree. A small pickup truck with a lawnmower on the bed was next to it.

"I don't think anyone will give us a ride even if we paid them," Danny stated.

"What about that taxi driver? He said we can call him anytime," Valerie suggested.

Danny reached into his back pocket and pulled out his wallet. He opened it and took out Pradeep's business card.

He was tempted to turn his phone back on, but that would be suicide. As soon as the signal was established, they would be sitting ducks. He was sure that Yuri and more men were already mobilizing.

Danny looked around and saw a Chinese restaurant, a burger joint, a flower shop, and a donut shop.

"WHY DID YOU SHOOT THE tires?" Dr. Tran screamed into his phone. "You could have killed them!"

"I had no choice but to stop the car. If it had reached San Diego, we'd be finished," the mysterious man replied.

"Where are they now?" Dr. Tran said, his voice rising in a panic.

"They ran into a strip mall. Do you want me to offer them a ride?"

"No, don't do that. They might suspect something. Just keep an eye on them and only intervene if more men come for them."

"TO THE CHINESE RESTAURANT. MAYBE they'll let us use their phone," Danny said, already walking toward it.

A hostess in her early twenties, wearing a tight-fitting red silk dress with a slit on the side, greeted them with a broad smile.

"My phone died. Can we use your phone to call a taxi?" Danny asked.

The hostess asked them to follow her to the cash register at the back of the restaurant. As they were walking past the tables, Danny saw a waiter with a tray of freshly-made pork steam buns, dumplings, and pan-fried noodles.

Danny picked up the receiver and dialed Pradeep's number, holding his breath as the phone rang. On the fourth ring, he answered.

"Hello."

"Pradeep. It's Danny."

"A great day to hear from you," Pradeep answered with enthusiasm in his voice.

"I need to ask a big favor. Can you come and get us? We need a ride back to San Diego."

"And where you might be, if I may ask?"

"Alpine."

The phone was silent for a few seconds. Danny worried that if Pradeep refused to come and fetch them, they'd be dead in the water.

"Your lucky day is indeed today. I just dropped off a passenger in El Cajon. Be there in twenty minutes."

"Great!"

TRUE TO HIS WORD, PRADEEP arrived on time. Danny and Valerie jumped in the back of his taxi and buckled themselves in.

"If I may ask, is Alpine a great place for sightseeing? What are you two doing here?" Pradeep asked, looking into the rearview mirror.

"It's a long story," Valerie said.

"Please take us to Balboa Park," Danny requested, relieved that he was finally on his way to meet Blake.

Seventeen

When Pradeep parked the taxi next to the curb on the side of the Natural History Museum, Danny felt confident. He had another fighting chance to save Elizabeth from getting killed. All he and Blake had to do was to pop the thumb drive into the laptop, scan their fingers and upload the information to the IP address given to them. The process wouldn't take more than ten minutes.

"We're pressed for time. I need to meet with Blake right away," Danny said, getting out of the taxi.

"Are we to wait here?" Pradeep asked.

"Please take her directly to Chicano Park in Logan Heights," Danny said, sticking his head through the passenger window.

Valerie reached for Danny's hand.

"Be careful. Dr. Adamson's hired guns are still out there looking for you," she said.

He looked directly into Valerie's worried eyes. He wanted to stay alive not only for Elizabeth, but especially for the lovely woman who had come back into his life.

"They're holding Elizabeth in an abandoned house just a few minutes from the bridge. You will receive a text from either me or Blake with the address as soon as the kidnappers receive the data," Danny replied, kissing her on the lips.

As the taxi pulled away from the curb, he realized that he truly cared for her and that the guilt he felt for loving someone other than Helen was unfounded. Danny needed someone too, and Valerie was the right woman for him. Maybe Helen's ghost was responsible for getting them together in the first place.

He thought to himself that if he survived the next hour, he would ask Valerie to come live with him. If Danny's heart was sliced in two, Valerie's name would be floating in the middle of it.

Danny passed by the fountain facing Park Boulevard as it spewed water freely up in the air. Parents sat lazily on the raised concrete border, watching their kids play in the ankle-deep water. He hoped by the next day, when the bright sunshine lit up the entire county, everyone would be safe in their homes.

Hurrying along the main promenade, he heard the sound of a street performer—a one-man band with a drum and cymbals on his back, a harmonica in his mouth, and a guitar in his hands. People were gathered around the performer, dropping coins in his hat. Next to the musician was an artist painting a caricature of a young woman sitting stiffly on the chair.

From a distance, he could already see the Baroque-style California Tower protruding from behind the buildings, embellished with high-relief sculptures on the top.

To his right was the lily pond. Lotus leaves floated on the clear water while orange and yellow koi skimmed for food at the surface. He caught a glimpse of the Botanical Building, a brown, tubular-shaped lattice with a dome in the middle, so unlike the gilded concrete buildings in the turn-of-the-century style.

He peeked to his left. He saw the El Cid statue, the Spanish war hero who sat valiantly on a horse, holding a spear while a couple posed for pictures, looking madly in love with each other. He checked Spreckels Organ Pavilion. The wing-shaped, open-air concert arena was empty. He hoped that Blake would appear from one of the nooks in the buildings so they could start uploading the data to the server. But no one was there.

Danny shielded his eyes from the sun with his right hand and looked up at the California Building—its dome gilded with mosaic tiles of green, blue, and white surrounding a yellow compass rose. He wished that it would point to where Blake was hiding. Seeing that the coast was clear, he sprinted up the wide stairs that led to the front entrance of the hundred-year-old structure.

AS SOON AS HE ENTERED the main lobby, Danny proceeded directly to the ticket booth to buy an entrance ticket that would allow him to climb all the way to the top of the tower. He was relieved to find that there was no line. The middle-aged clerk with light brown hair and graying roots looked at Danny with a bored expression on her face. He pulled out a twenty-dollar bill and handed it to the woman.

Ticket in hand, he skirted around stone sculptures, turned his phone on and inserted the headphone into his ear.

It only took him a few minutes to get to the top of the California Tower. Danny was walking around a group of out-of-towners when he overheard a man with a Southern drawl ask the tour guide how California got its name. The tour guide said the name came from a mythical place that was taken from a popular novel published in the 16th century.

Danny proceeded directly to the balcony. He looked down at the courtyard and traced his eyes over the tree-tops with downtown San Diego's skyline in the background. Shifting his eyes slightly to the left, he marveled at the immaculately manicured Alcazar Garden that was lined with green hedges and mosaic-designed benches.

He pressed Blake's speed dial. "Where are you?"

"I'm hiding in the trees."

"I can't see you. I'm up here now."

OK . . . I'm going to an open space to wave at you."

"OK."

Danny concentrated on what was in front of him but after a few frustrating minutes, he could not see Blake. The area where Blake was standing was thick with trees. Locating him seemed impossible. He pointed his phone at the area where Blake should be and took a picture. Using his thumb and forefinger, he expanded the area. He scanned through the image until finally finding Blake's light-skinned arms in between the trees directly in front of him. A twinge of relief tickled his stomach knowing that in less than fifteen minutes, their dilemma would finally be over.

"I just spotted you!" Danny said, excitement in his voice. "Wait for me. I'm coming down there."

Danny had just taken his eyes away from the trees. His knees weakened when he saw Yuri on the Cabrillo Bridge running in his direction. He loved that high-arched bridge, but at that moment wished it had never been built at all.

Danny thought of quickly going down the stairs and hiding in one of the many hidden chambers of the museum. He glanced at his wristwatch to see that it was already 6:15 p.m. They had only 45 minutes left to resolve their dilemma. Getting downstairs and exiting through the front or the rear doors was out of the question, Danny realized. Yuri could spot him. If that happened, Danny wouldn't be able to outrun him. The ponytailed man was far more agile than Danny and determined to capture him.

His only option was to let Yuri pass by, and when he was far away, to quickly get down undetected and join up with Blake.

Looking straight down at the front entrance to see if Ponytail had already run past. A cold sweat broke on Danny's forehead when he saw Yuri looking straight up back at him.

Yuri flashed a smug smile, then ran up the stairs and entered the main lobby.

Danny was trapped in the building—climbing down was his only option. He was sure that the man with the ponytail who had been chasing him since yesterday would make it up in a matter of minutes. Yuri would not leave until his prey was found. Besides, Danny could not hide in the building indefinitely because the clock was ticking. At precisely 7:00 p.m., Elizabeth would drown if he and Blake could not fulfill the kidnapper's demands.

His only escape was to rappel down. To do that, he would have to make it down a fifty-foot drop from the tower's balcony to the California Building's roof. He walked back to the balcony and looked down for the best way to get down. The drop was forbidding. He could climb down by stepping on the low relief sculpture near the top of the tower but there was the obstacle of scaling down the smooth surface of the wall that ran straight down from where he stood.

Danny was in a great quandary.

He couldn't figure out how to get down without breaking his legs or cracking his head on the roof.

Danny looked around and noticed two long cloth banners just below the balcony. He reached over, pulled the yellow banner and unhooked it from the metal rod where it was hanging. The tour guide approached him, threatening to call security if he didn't stop what he was doing. Danny ignored her. He reached for the blue banner and tied it to the end of the yellow one in a square knot. Confident the two banners wouldn't slip off each other, he tied the other end of the yellow banner onto the balcony's wrought iron banister. He tugged on the knotted fabric several times. Assured that it would hold his weight, he threw his leg over the railing.

"Stop what you're doing!" the tour guide shouted as the group of tourists she was leading watched with stunned faces.

Danny ignored her warning. Instead, he dropped the banners over the railing. Wrapping the cloth around his buttocks, he began rappelling down the tower—hoping that his daring plan would work. If he failed, he might meet the same fate as those people who suffered in the devices displayed at the Torture Museum just in front of him. Getting captured by Yuri wasn't an option.

Danny kicked away from the wall and released the grip on the banner. The rough cloth scraped his hips. The view from the top of the tower was dizzying as he dangled at least a hundred feet from the ground. If his hands slipped or if he miscalculated the amount of slack he needed to let go, he would tumble all the way down and plunge directly into the unforgiving concrete. It would be an instant death.

YURI WAS RUNNING UP THE stairs when, from out of the corner of his eye, he noticed the yellow banner dangling outside. Suspecting that something wasn't right, he rushed to the window and looked down. To his surprise, he saw

Danny lowering himself down the tower at a steady pace. He grabbed the banner and began shaking it, hoping Danny would lose his grip and fall all the way down.

DANNY WAS ABOUT FIFTEEN FEET off the ground when he felt the banner shaking. The rough surface of the banner began shearing the palms of his hands. He found it odd. At first, he thought the knot was coming apart. With a quick upward glance to investigate what was wrong, he saw Yuri looking down with a pistol aimed at him.

Worried that the first shot would hit him directly in his head, Danny hopped from side to side, hoping to avoid the bullet's path.

PONYTAIL PULLED THE TRIGGER.

DANNY FELT SOMETHING ZOOM PAST the side of his face. Down below, he saw the pink, bushy tail of a tranquilizer dart. The same type used to temporarily paralyze out-of-control animals. The man was trying to incapacitate him instead of killing him.

He wanted to loosen his grip on the banner and jump, but he was still hanging at least fifteen feet off the ground. He'd certainly break his ankles, stopping him from climbing down to flee Yuri's pursuit.

Not thinking and just reacting to the desperation of his situation, he slackened his hold on the banner. Gravity immediately did its work—Danny was dropping like a rock.

About five feet above the roof, Danny wrapped the banner around his arm to stop the fall. He felt a tug just as his acceleration ceased. He looked up to find that the banner was ripping apart from the top, and he was tumbling down uncontrollably.

As soon as his feet touched the rooftop, he rolled to his side to absorb the impact. His left shoulder smashed hard against the solid surface. Danny quickly got up and ignored the pain, shooting a quick glance up to see whether Yuri was still aiming the gun at him.

The balcony was empty.

Trying to capitalize on his lead, Danny laid his stomach on top of the facade and swung his legs down. He noticed Junípero Serra's statue standing proudly, its sad eyes looking straight at him. He whispered an apology to the founder of the California missions for scuffing all the excellent artwork on the front of the building. Clawing his fingers into the curves of the stone ornamentations for stability and carefully planting his foot down on the mantle, Danny took one step at a time like a rock climber. A few minutes later, he made it all the way down to the front entrance, relieved at the thought that he had plenty of time to get to Blake.

THROUGH THE WINDOWS OF THE California Tower, Yuri watched Danny run across the courtyard toward the bridge, pissed that he had gotten away. He glanced at his phone to check the time. He had only half an hour left, and if he didn't get to Danny or Blake before the data was uploaded, Dr. Adamson would punish him for his incompetence. He sent another text asking Igor to get to his location right away for backup. Still, there was no answer.

Arriving at the Cabrillo Bridge where he had seen Danny disappear, Yuri frantically searched for any sign of him. He sprinted down the hill, passing by tall trees when out of the corner of his eye, he saw fresh footprints on the soft soil leading down under the bridge. A cruel grin spread across his face, confident that he'd capture Danny and Blake. He readied his tranquilizer gun and followed the trail of footprints.

BLAKE WAS STANDING NEXT TO a eucalyptus tree with the dedicated laptop in his hand when Danny arrived.

"Come on, let's go!" Blake urged.

Danny pulled the thumb drive from his front pocket and thrust it into the USB port. Blake flipped the computer screen up. A window popped on the screen with instructions asking for his thumbprint. Danny placed his thumb on the touchpad. The system could not recognize the information so he shifted his thumb slightly to the left. He could see the dots blinking over the key areas of the whorls and loops in his thumb as the computer compared it with the information stored in the remote server. After a few tense seconds, the thumbprint screen turned green, authenticating his identity. Quickly, he punched in his password.

"Now, your turn," Danny said.

Blake placed his thumb on the scanner. A few seconds later, the green light flashed. Blake had just entered the first four digits of his ten-digit password when Danny and Blake heard popping sounds. Tranquilizer darts tore through the tree trunks and sliced the low hanging leaves in half. Danny and Blake hit the ground fast.

Danny searched his immediate surroundings for cover, but there was no safe place to hide. To his astonishment, he saw Ponytail rushing over to where they stood, his pistol aimed at them as if they were prized game animals.

"Finish your password and hit upload now!" Danny directed.

Blake set the laptop on the ground and entered the last remaining numbers. As soon as the confirm button turned green, he pressed the send button.

"We're good!" Blake confirmed.

Not wanting to waste precious seconds, Blake closed the laptop and clutched it tight to his chest to save it from being taken by Yuri.

"This way!" Danny exclaimed, pointing to the wooded area near the bridge.

They were speeding down the hill when Blake's arm bumped into a tree trunk. The laptop slipped from his hands and went tumbling down into the shrubs.

"Fuck!" Blake cursed under his breath.

Immediately, Blake was on his knees, searching for the laptop.

Because the data to be uploaded was 25 gigabytes and the spotty cell-phone signal was only 3G or less, completing the task could take several minutes.

Worried that the laptop might be destroyed if the man with the ponytail snatched it away from them, Danny cried out, "Save the laptop and run! Don't worry about me!"

Blake folded the laptop and ran as fast as he could. Danny looked at his friend, not knowing if he would ever see him again.

"WHERE'S THE THUMB DRIVE? OR I'll shoot you down," Yuri demanded, pointing the gun at him.

"Fuck you!" Danny shouted back.

To Danny's surprise, Yuri was holding a yellow gun with a flat tip that looked like it was made of hard plastic. He immediately recognized it as a stun gun. For it to work correctly, the two projectiles attached to the wires needed to make contact with any part of the body so that the five million volts of energy would disable its target. With Yuri at striking distance and with no place for Danny to run, dodging the other contact was his only hope.

"Don't move!" Yuri ordered.

Danny stared at the man who was going to shoot him. The tip of the gun was less than ten feet away from his face. Danny's surveyed his immediate surrounding looking for a way out or for a miracle to appear, but it was just him and the villain.

"Just give me the drive and this will be all over," Yuri commanded.

"Why would I do that? You'll kill me anyway," Danny snapped back.

Yuri's eyes narrowed in frustration.

"Give it to me or I will take you to the Torture Museum myself and lock you in the iron maiden. You'll be begging me to take the thumb drive from you."

Pretending that he was desperate for his life, Danny raised his hands up in the air but kept his eyes glued on Yuri's hand. The laser sight centered on his chest.

Yuri's hand twitched. A loud pop followed.

Reacting quickly, Danny turned his body sideways. One of the probes hit his arm. He felt a stinging sensation, but the other probe bounced off his chest.

Danny lunged forward, grabbed Yuri's wrist and slammed his fist into the man's right eye.

Moving quickly, Danny grabbed the stun gun from Yuri, but Yuri seemed to detect his intention right away. Yuri swung the edge of his hand and karate-chopped the gun away from Danny's possession. It flew several feet away into the bushes.

From his waistband, Yuri took out a brass knuckle. He flashed Danny a menacing smile and started to wave his knuckle wildly in front of Danny's face like a prizefighter would do with gloved hands.

Yuri lurched at him with a punch. As Yuri took a forward swing, Danny grabbed Yuri's arm and pulled it towards him. Yuri's face collided directly into Danny's elbow. Yuri hollered in pain but quickly readjusted his position, now within striking distance.

Yuri balled his fingers for another strike but missed landing a direct hit, only grazing the side of Danny's jaw. With a strong grip, Danny grabbed Yuri's wrist and deflected the blow away from him, causing Yuri to lose balance. Using his right hand, Danny grabbed Ponytail by the collar and threw him on the ground. But as Yuri was falling down, he reached for Danny. With his fingertips, Yuri hooked Danny's shoulder, pulling Danny with him.

Danny was caught unprepared when Yuri managed to get on top of him. Yuri began punching Danny in the face. Danny shielded his face with his arms. Wanting to stop Yuri from turning his face into a punching bag, he wrapped his arms around Yuri. The lull gave Danny an opportunity to roll over on top of Yuri. Danny wrapped his arm around his opponent's neck. For the first time in the fight, Danny had the upper hand and could cut off the air going down Yuri's windpipe to knock the man unconscious. Yuri's neck veins bulged, stringed tight as if ready to snap. Keeping the chokehold going for a few more seconds was tiring on his arms but Danny held his position.

Yuri didn't give up. With both hands, he reached over his head and pulled Danny's left hand down, breaking Danny's grip before it would have finished him.

Desperate, Yuri lifted off the ground and twisted away from Danny. Danny's arm clamping over Yuri's chest slackened. Pressing his head on the ground and using his feet, he pushed himself upwards. Yuri was able to wiggle out.

Danny bent his knees and tried to use his legs as a wedge between him and Yuri, but it was futile. Yuri overpowered him and like a snake squeezed himself behind Danny. Anticipating a chokehold, Danny lifted his shoulders and pointed his chin down to shield his trachea from getting crushed. He could feel Yuri's arm pressing down on his chin. It was difficult to fill his lungs with much needed oxygen through his bent windpipe.

Danny was desperate for a way out as Yuri's hold on him was getting firmer with each second, Yuri's leg wrapped around his torso like a python. With each passing second, the air in Danny's lungs was becoming stale. As the carbon increased and the oxygen decreased, his skin became pale. His vision of the surroundings was quickly becoming sepia tone.

He tried to keep his chin down and shoulders up, but it was just too exhausting. He reached behind to pull Yuri's arm off him, but it was just simply too difficult. He couldn't find the energy to keep himself from losing consciousness— and possibly his life.

With Danny's back on the side of the slope, he could feel his hips on the uneven ground. Through the panicked haze in his mind, he quickly formulated a plan to escape. He took his hands off the man's arms and grabbed Yuri by the hips.

Using all his remaining energy, Danny lifted his buttocks off the ground and pulled Yuri sideways. Gravity did the rest of the work. Soon, the two of them were rolling down the hill. While going down, Danny flattened his hands and shoved them between his neck and Yuri's arm and lifted it off him. Finally, he was able to get himself free from the death grip.

Soon, fresh air was filling his lungs. Danny desperately tried to push Yuri away from him as they rolled down, but Yuri was determined to hang on to him like a leech sucking blood. The drop was getting steeper, and the two men were going down faster and faster, and out of control.

When they finally rolled to a stop, Yuri wasn't moving. Danny saw Yuri's arms and legs spread wide—a sharp tree stump was protruding through his chest, dripping with bright red blood. Yuri was lifeless.

Danny immediately felt pain shoot up his spine. His lower back had slammed against a rock jutting from the ground. He couldn't move his legs. He attempted to get up but was unable to do it. His phone beeped. There was a message in his inbox. With his free hand, he retrieved his phone from his front pocket. Holding the phone over his face, he was glad to see the address where Elizabeth was being held displayed on the screen. The data transmission was successful after all. In agony, he painstakingly copied the address and forwarded it to Valerie.

He was about to dial 9-1-1 when two men in black boots and tactical pants blocked his view of the yellowing sky. Thinking that Dr. Adamson had called for reinforcements, he resolved that his life was over. One of the men reached for his arm, holding a syringe filled with an unknown substance. Danny tried to resist but the man's partner pinned him to the ground. Danny thought he heard instructions spoken in rapid English with an eastern European accent, but with the 163 freeway so close and the noise from the cars whizzing by so loud, he just couldn't be sure what he'd heard.

Danny felt the needle poke the muscle on his upper arm.

His peripheral vision began to blur. Now, he wasn't sure if the address he received was bogus. He might not have saved Elizabeth from getting killed and he could soon be dead.

Just as he was about to lose consciousness, he saw Blake looking down at him with a serious look on his face.

EIGHTEEN

VALERIE PULLED THE DOOR LATCH, pushed the taxi door open and slid herself out. Aside from a homeless person pushing a shopping cart filled with all his earthly possessions and a woman playing with her two small children, Chicano Park was virtually empty. She walked under the concrete bridge and looked up at the cars zooming above. For the hundredth time, she checked her phone hoping a message was already waiting with the address.

Chicano Park was at the bottom of the foot of Coronado Bridge in the center of Barrio Logan. Artists had painted the pylons supporting the bridge, featuring the struggles of Mexican-Americans in the United States. Valerie looked up at the yellow, red and purple brush strokes depicting Montezuma's outstretched arms, hoping the Aztec emperor would whisper Elizabeth's location.

At precisely 6:50 p.m., Valerie's phone vibrated. She looked at the screen and saw Elizabeth's location.

"Come on, let's go!" Valerie snapped, jumping back into the taxi.

Pradeep punched the street address on the GPS, stepped on the gas and yelped, "We're only less than half a mile."

Though it should only take them less than five minutes to reach the address, it was impossible to go fast enough through the heavy traffic on Logan Avenue. It was rush hour and commuters were eager to get home. With each wasted minute, Valerie's pulse quickened in anxiety.

The traffic was practically at a standstill. They were at least a tenth of a mile away. Valerie looked around her to see if any cars were coming. Seeing that it was clear, she pushed the door open and jumped out. "I'm running to the house. Follow me!" she shouted, looking down at her phone for guidance.

The place was an old abandoned home. Valerie barged through the front door. Immediately, she saw the water line just below Elizabeth's nose as she struggled to breathe.

She exhaled though her mouth, bubbles rising to the surface as tears streamed down her cheeks. She tried to free herself but to no avail. Her feet were chained to the floor. Quickly, Valerie reached over the top of the tank and tried to push water away from Elizabeth's face for her much-needed air.

Valerie searched for the tube filling the tank with water but couldn't find it. Then she saw a lead pipe propped against the wall. Using all her strength, she struck the glass tank hard. A crack formed where the tip of the pipe made contact. She swung again, hitting the same spot. After the fifth try, the glass broke, sending hundreds of gallons gushing onto the floor.

Elizabeth was finally free.

Nineteen

Danny opened his eyes. The light streaming from the large bay window blinded him. He turned away from the bright light and immediately felt that his neck was stiff. With his right hand, he began touching his stomach and his thighs, curious if the men who had drugged him had tied him up. He was glad to see that his legs were unbound. As his eyes were adjusting to the brightness in the room, he noticed Valerie lying on the sofa about ten feet away from him, a thin white blanket pulled up to her chest.

Fearing they were both locked in the room, he wondered where their captors were keeping them. He lifted his head, but it felt heavy. He swung his legs towards the edge of the bed wanting to get up, ruffling the sheets and causing the bed frame to creak.

Valerie woke up from the noise.

"Stay still. You might fall out of bed," Valerie said, getting up from the sofa.

"How long have we been here?" Danny mumbled.

"Eighteen hours. But you were mostly asleep."

"Were we captured?" Danny asked, fearing for the worse.

"No . . . you're in the hospital."

"Who were those men who drugged me?"

"Paramedics. Blake called the police and an ambulance as soon as the data was transmitted."

Danny was relieved with her news.

"And Elizabeth?"

"She's safe with Blake."

"What did the doctor say?" Danny asked, wondering if there was extensive damage.

"You banged the back of your head hard on the ground, but you should be OK. The doctor was just here five hours ago with your CT scan results. Looks like you had a minor concussion. He said rest will do you good," Valerie reassured him, reaching for the control and raising the head of the bed.

With the side effects of the pain medications that were still in his system, and since he had been lying in bed unconscious for almost a day, Danny felt queasy. He sat up to relieve his sore back. Valerie sat next to him, holding his shoulders to block him from falling forward and hitting his face. Danny turned his attention to the window. The cars along the freeway were bumper to bumper. Red lights flashed as the drivers tapped on their brakes. The blue Pacific Ocean glistened in the background. He imagined the soothing sound of the sea down below. He couldn't wait to get back on his sailboat and cruise around the bay, reaching all the way to the tip of Point Loma. He missed looking at the mainsail as it curved and puffed, filling with the wind pushing it forward.

"What happened to the man who was trying to kill me?" Danny said as he looked at Valerie.

"He's dead."

"What about Dr. Adamson? We should call the police."

Valerie shook her head. "Right after the data was uploaded, he hopped on a plane and fled the country. He's somewhere in Europe now, but Interpol was already alerted. Dr. Tran was behind Elizabeth's kidnapping. The police picked him up yesterday for questioning. The phone recovered from the man who was trying to kill you apparently had been recording Dr. Tran's conversations with the kidnappers. He wanted the data uploaded to the server so it could discredit Dr. Adamson and help him win the contract."

Danny bowed down, fighting off his dizziness. As he tried to analyze Valerie's news, he couldn't believe what he had just heard. Two of his fellow scientists were behind everything that had happened in the last 48 hours.

"Thank you for staying with me," Danny said warmly, reaching for Valerie's hand.

Valerie's face was expressionless as she slowly pulled her hand away. She shifted her gaze away from him and said, "I don't think we're meant for each other, Danny."

Danny was perplexed with her declaration.

"Why do you say that? You know these last two days have been so meaningful to us."

"You were calling Helen all night. I think you still haven't gotten over her," Valerie muttered, as tiny drops of tears formed in the corner of her eyes. "I can't compete with a dead woman anymore."

"You're the one I want."

"But we can't go on living like this."

"That was my unconscious mind. It has nothing to do with my reality," Danny assured her.

Danny was surprised to feel Valerie's hand lacking the warmth he had always known. He could beg her all day to stay with him, but he understood where she was coming from. It was hard to love someone who had half of his heart still attached to his dead wife.

"Valerie, it's not too late. We could still be together."

"Why is this happening to us?" Valerie questioned. This time, she was looking straight at Danny.

Valerie said nothing further and kissed him on the forehead. For the first time, Valerie's kiss felt formal. He wanted her to be near him, but she was right. The woman he'd always wanted was only a few inches away from him, but he knew that his heart wasn't all hers. Valerie could never be happy if his mind was still unconsciously thinking of Helen. Valerie might be right, he thought, and the only way to keep her sanity intact was for her to stay away from him.

Valerie got up from the bed.

Her voice trembled as she looked at him. "The way we came together . . . I don't think it's meant to be. These past few days seem like some sort of dream, but not something that can last. You know, it probably would do both of us good if we just forget that we've ever met."

His heart began to thump in his chest from the fear of losing her. He wanted to reason and tell her that they were meant for each other. To put logic into her head. To tell her that they had a good thing going. But Danny doubted if convincing her to love him was the right thing to do. If they had a future together, then she had to decide for herself.

SHE PICKED UP HER HANDBAG sitting on the couch and headed for the door. Danny tried to get out of bed to stop her, but his aching muscles wouldn't let him. She reached for the brass doorknob, cold in her hand just like the cold, empty feeling inside her chest. She pulled the door open, but stopped halfway as if contemplating whether she was making a big mistake and should run back into Danny's arms. Her eyes began to fill with tears, and her chest became heavy.

"Valerie!" Danny cried out.

She ignored his plea. Instead, she walked out of the room and forever out of Danny's life.

EPILOGUE

DANNY WAS WALKING AT A slow pace. The ground was firm under his feet. The sweet smell of freshly cut grass still hung in the air.

A month after the kidnapping incident, he was back on his feet again.

The grounds at the cemetery were empty, except for a woman who looked to be in her late seventies sitting by the grave of a loved one. Danny had seen that exact scene many times before. He had been visiting Helen's grave at least once a month for two years now. He looked to the top of the hill and zeroed in on a tree that had served as his marker for where Helen was laid to rest.

Helen's pink granite gravestone was shiny. He could still vividly remember that day when he heard the news that she had died in a car crash while driving alone on a dark two-lane highway, heading home from a meeting.

Holding a dozen roses in his hands, he read the inscription: "A wife to one and a friend to many."

Danny carefully placed the bouquet of flowers upright in the holder. With his bare hands, he pushed aside the fallen twigs and blades of grass that had blown over the gravestone. He squatted and spread his knees apart.

Looking down at Helen's tomb, he began to speak, "I think you already know what has been going on between Valerie and me. She's your good friend and I want to be with her. You are not here now, but I'll always love you. If your wish is for me to stay single until we meet again, then I will do so. Helen, please tell me what to do."

Tears began to flow down Danny's cheeks. His eyes reddened and it became difficult to breathe through his clogged nose. He was silent as he waited for a sign from Helen. The wind blew. Dried leaves cartwheeled across the green grass. The air became cooler. A few minutes later, he felt a hand on his shoulder.

Curious who was standing behind him, he turned around. There wasn't anything in his vicinity but the tree next to him. A small olive branch snapped and fell by his feet. He picked it up and brought it closer to face. As he was inspecting its narrow leaves, he soon understood that it was a peace offering from Helen. Then he heard her say, *"Go now, my love. You must let me go. You showed me a good life while I was alive, loved me for what I was and that was enough for any woman like me to have experienced in a lifetime. We are now in different dimensions, and it is now time for you to carry on. I promise that I will not visit you in your sleep anymore or disturb you in your waking hours."*

Maybe it was just his imagination or maybe it was really Helen talking to him. No matter what it was, what he heard was genuine. He felt a sudden lightness in his chest, and the weight of guilt flew away with the wind. It was done. Helen had given her blessing.

Danny knew that the only way to live in the present was to keep moving forward. Helen was gone—that was a fact. His daily struggle of carrying the guilt of leaving her for another woman was truly over. He was free to go. Danny knelt next to the tomb, imagined her blue-grey eyes, placed his finger on his lips, and touched the shiny marker that read, "Helen Glass Maglaya."

BUILT ON THE SIDE OF a hill overlooking downtown San Diego, Blake and Elizabeth's Craftsman-style house stood proudly in the early afternoon light.

Danny approached the porch and rang the doorbell. When the door swung open, he saw Elizabeth standing at the door, her long curly blonde hair neatly brushed. She spread her arms wide and stepped towards him. Her embrace was tight and full of platonic love.

"Thank you for everything you did to save me," Elizabeth said, pulling away from him.

"It's my fault. You shouldn't have been involved with my invention," Danny apologized.

"Shh . . . do not say that. You and Blake are helping save the world. There's nothing nobler. Besides, I'm alive. Come on, everyone's in the back."

There must have been at least 50 guests standing in the backyard with drinks in their hands when Danny arrived. He saw Blake standing at his tiki bar.

"I'm glad you made it," Blake said, relief painted on his face.

"How could I miss Elizabeth's bridal shower?"

"The guys will stay here by the hut while the gals do their bridal shower thing inside. They want to corral us all in one spot, so we all don't head straight to the strip club."

"Any news with Dr. Adamson?"

"He's still hiding somewhere," Blake said, handing Danny an AMF cocktail.

"And Dr. Tran?"

"He's out on bail, but he's finished. Like your drink, he's Adios Motherfucker from the program. I still can't believe he was behind the kidnapping."

As Danny took a sip of his refreshing drink, he remembered that special day when he was the groom and Blake was his best man. Back then, Blake was single, and he was the one getting married. Now their roles were reversed.

To Danny's surprise, he saw Valerie standing among the other future bridesmaids across the yard.

"A margarita, please," Danny requested.

HE FELT A LIGHTNESS IN his being as he approached Valerie, as if he was being released from some kind of captivity. She looked elegant in her white summer dress and high heels. She made eye contact with Danny and gave him a slight smile.

"Your favorite drink," Danny said, giving her the glass.

"I didn't think you'd show up," Valerie remarked, the look in her eyes revealing she was glad to see him.

"I was just thinking the same. I thought you wouldn't mind if I came."

"The more, the merrier." Valerie smiled at his comment.

They were silent for a moment, not knowing what to say to each other next.

A few seconds later, Danny broke the awkward silence.

"I stopped by Helen's grave before coming here. I told her about us. While I was kneeling on the grass, I—"

"You felt a hand touch your shoulder?" Valerie interrupted.

"How'd you know that?" Danny asked, wide-eyed.

"Just as I was getting out of my car earlier, I thought she did the same thing to me. I even thought I heard her whisper something in my ear."

"I think it was a sign for both of us. She's letting us go."

It was then that the guilty feelings that had been dragging them down were gone. They needed to grab the brass ring on the last go-around of the carousel of their tumultuous affair.

"Valerie, there's no reason why we shouldn't follow what we truly feel for each other."

Danny knew that Valerie wanted to be with him as much as he did. The past was just that—the past—and it was only their future together that lay ahead of them. It was time to act on their desires and to follow what their hearts dictated.

Danny placed his forefinger on her lips, stopping her from uttering another word. There wasn't much more to say, he thought. Sorry was for yesterday. Sorry needed to be buried with the mistakes of the past. Today was for forgiveness, for understanding, and to wipe the slate clean.

VALERIE THOUGHT TO HERSELF, "HOW could I push this man away when I melt whenever he flashes his dimpled smile?"

BLAKE BLASTED DANCE MUSIC FROM the eighties. The guests converged in the middle of the grass. Danny glanced in Valerie's direction. She turned to him at the same time. They smiled at each other, half-embarrassed like two teenagers meeting at the school dance for the first time.

"Will you dance with me?" Danny proposed.

Valerie reached for his hand. Just as they were walking towards the green grass to dance the afternoon away, they looked behind them. Blake and Elizabeth were watching them with amused eyes. As music and laughter filled the air, Valerie raised herself up on tiptoes to kiss Danny on the lips. He smiled at her sudden impulse. With that act, her kiss sealed what they had felt for each other all along.

THANK YOU

It is my pleasure that you enjoyed reading my novel *Somewhere in San Diego*.

One of the best rewards an author could ever have is when readers tell their friends about the book they'd just read. I'd appreciate it if you tell others you know who are book lovers about your experience reading my novel.

I'd be so grateful if you post a review where you bought this book or if you have an account on Goodreads, Amazon or if you have a personal blog.

WEBSITE:
Dennismacaraeg.com

SOCIAL MEDIA:
Facebook.com/dennismacaraegauthor
Twitter.com/DennisMac2015
Instagram.com/Denniswriter
Medium.com/@DennisMac2015